Mary Jones was born in Aberystwyth and was educated at St Padarn's Convent School there and later at Sheffield University. Since 1969 she has been Lecturer in English at the University of Ulster.

Resistance

Mary Jones

THE
BLACKSTAFF
PRESS

First published in 1985
by The Blackstaff Press Limited
3 Galway Park, Dundonald, Belfast BT16 0AN
with the assistance of
The Arts Council of Northern Ireland

Printed in Northern Ireland by
The Universities Press Limited

British Library Cataloguing in Publication Data

Jones, Mary
Resistance.
I. Title
823'.914[F]   PR6060.O55

ISBN 0 85640 336 9 (hardback)
0 85640 330 X (paperback)

To D.H. Gibb

CHAPTER ONE

The man at the desk looked as if he didn't sleep very much. He also looked as though he might be able to see in the dark.

From the way he stared, you would have thought I was sleep-walking towards him. Clearly, he shared my uncertainty about what I was doing there: about what I was going to do next, he seemed even more apprehensive.

Living in that gloom, I thought, you'd need to be able to see in the dark.

'*Mae'n boeth iawn, ond yw hi?*' he said (instead of whatever he had been on the point of saying).

'Pardon?'

The bulging eyes clouded, but they were still too slippery to hold. He enquired in toneless, formal English whether I could be helped. Close to, his pupils, set in an almost transparent jelly, reminded me of frogspawn.

'A single was it, madam?'

Said like that, it was more suspicious than a double.

He turned his back on me and glanced along the rows of empty pigeon-holes. There were keys dangling beside them, lolling like tongues from vacuous mouths, and I fancied the slots were starting to roll under the little black balls of his eyes, like a roulette wheel speeding up.

'Are you alright?'

It was just the effect of the revolving doors on the way in, I told him, making me giddy. And the atrocious heat in his part of Wales, I added more sourly, for there had been irritability in his voice – I was neither young enough, nor old enough, to arouse any real concern in him. Neither, it seemed, was I worth listening to – he gazed deafly at my hands clutching the desk, as though he were making a mental note of the exact spot where my fingerprints were.

1

He consulted the book again, took down a key, and returned to his scrutiny.

'Perhaps if you heat the page, I'll come up like magic.'

'Pardon?' It was a rebuke to frivolity merely. 'When was this booking made, madam?'

'Yesterday.'

'Ah.' I had evidently been withholding information.

Reluctantly, as though it unlocked the magazine store, he released the key.

'Are you quite sure you want me to have this, now?'

'Madam is staying for. . .? How long is madam staying?'

The entrance hall yawned like a vault around the two of us. All that caught my eye was the glass of the doors, glinting as they slowly revolved, like the blinding facets of a crystal ball.

'I couldn't say for sure, yet.'

'No, of course you couldn't.'

'Maybe till the fourteenth of September. Maybe.'

He scribbled something, leaving a note for the receptionist perhaps, pulling back long-sightedly. Casually, absently, he enquired: 'And do you have your passport there please, madam?'

'I beg your pardon?'

Our smiles were forcibly benign.

'Your passport?'

'I haven't got one.' I spoke mildly; this could be an easy way of leaving without having to make any decision to leave. But the next second I was hit by all the helpless frustration I had accumulated over a hundred such interrogations. 'I may be under a misunderstanding but I thought I was still in Britain. Free country and so on.'

He didn't even wince. 'I am merely asking madam for some means of identification.'

'I'm sorry, I don't carry identification papers. For the same reason.'

'A cheque card, perhaps?' he suggested with all the lingering triumph of Jeeves producing a trump card for Wooster. 'Or even a driving licence would do.'

'I've given up driving and they don't like you using cheque cards

2

when you're on the dole. Sorry.' I was never going to learn not to apologise.

To my surprise he sighed, apparently in defeat, and swung the register round to face me.

'Would you sign here please?'

'Yes, of course.' I was so willing, I wrote my name where the date should have been, and then patently forgot my address for a good few seconds. 'Is that alright?'

'Thank you, Mrs. . . er. . . Miss Thomas.' He looked up grimly. 'One might almost have thought you were Welsh.'

This I treated as his little joke.

'The door's locked at eleven and there is no night porter.'

'Locked?'

'Locked.'

'That affair?'

'That affair.'

'How on earth do you lock up that affair?'

'Very effectively, I can assure you.' His grimness melted into suave self-assurance. 'From a security point of view, those doors could not be bettered.'

'I can see that. I'm surprised anyone ever gets in.' The carpet lapped, a mottled grey ocean, around the lonely reef of the desk where we clung. 'I can see I'm one of the chosen few. If not the chosen one.'

'Oh, they don't discriminate.' He closed the register with a nasty satisfaction. 'Crooks have been known to get just as tangled up in them as the police.'

There was an awkward silence, sultry and dismal.

'I suppose madam will be requiring a key?'

My sweaty hand uncurled, like a child's caught in possession of illicit sweets. 'But you've just given me one.'

'That's the key to your room. We usually also give residents a key to one of the hotel's side doors, in case they want to come in late.'

'Oh – no thanks.'

'Just as you wish.' He lifted the phone and asked someone to conduct me to my room.

'It's quite alright, I can manage,' I assured him and bore my case away. After a while I had to come back to ask where the lifts were, and by then a porter was loitering intentionally by.

'Lifts?' His large palms spread like a picture of Christ ascending. 'She wants lifts,' he called to the porter. 'They're like your passport, madam; quite redundant.'

'Like me too then.'

He seemed to cheer up at that, relieved perhaps at the suggestion of redundancy money; he might, after all, have been worrying about payment ever since I had mentioned staying a month, and the dole.

I showed little interest in the room I was shown, simply sat on the bed waiting for the porter to go. When he hovered, I thought he was going to reprimand me for abusing the bed by sitting on it, and I grew so anxious planning my indignation that I forgot about a tip until he'd gone.

It was a tall, narrow room, utterly without character. Apart from the incongruously lavish carpet with its blue and gold pattern, it had more affinity with a hospital than a hotel. For some reason the bare white walls had been coated with gloss paint: they and the white basin gleamed with health and sterility: even the white bedspread bristled with cleanliness. But there was, at least, at the end of the bed, a French window and a balcony.

It was as stuffy outside as in, and it turned out not to be a balcony after all. Just a rough wooden platform running the length of the building. There was another on the floor above, and I could see between the gaps in the planks at my feet, as through Venetian blinds, that there was also one on the floor below. It was a rude system of ways that were boxed in to handrail level, and set so closely one on top of the other, they were more like a series of tunnels than balconies. They also ran along the wings at right angles to the block I was in, and along the wing opposite, enclosing the back yard I overlooked, and buckling crazily at opposite corners into steps that spiralled down into the puddles flooding the yard.

With all that scaffolding outside, the blue and gold of the carpet were all I was ever going to see of the sky and the sun.

4

Well, it wasn't what I'd had in mind. Most decidedly not. Wretched girl at the tourist office. The moment she refused to handle the brochure because her nails were wet, I should have guessed that she would interpret 'impersonal but quiet' as large and empty. No interest in her job at all.

And here I was – stranded – in some starless wonder, in a market town in Powys. Well, I wasn't staying. I just wasn't, and that was all there was to it. Well leave then. How? Hitch. Just hitch anywhere, like a student. Dear God, you didn't see people hitching in tweed coats and suitcases. And whatever was the matter with my thumb-nail? A distinct purplish hue where the half-moon should have been – reminiscent of the purple that radishes sometimes have, which puts you off eating them some-how.

Sharp as an electric shock, something streaked across my jaw. It made me remember that I should have found out the times of meals. The back of the door offered me instructions on fire-drill merely; other irrational, but likely places, like inside the ward-robe, offered me nothing at all. I would have to go back down-stairs.

But now I couldn't even find any stairs. The place was a maze of corridors where you were forever coming up against culs-de-sac, or doors that led only onto the wooden superstructure outside. It had started to rain, a light mizzle, dampening the wood but not enough to make any visible impression on the puddles below. Not enough to cool the air either.

I kept retracing my steps down passages that seemed to go off at tangents from one another, quite arbitrarily, until I became hope-lessly tangled up. Little tempting branch-roads were constantly opening up too, narrower, lower, holes in the wall almost, as though miners following a coal-seam had suddenly blasted through into a forgotten, unchartered tunnel they had dug a century earlier in a different direction. The place abounded with their uneven, accidental intersections.

Suddenly, I hit the void of the entrance hall. (There didn't seem to be any stairs as such – just sloping passages and intermittent steps.) It was like coming out into a cathedral cave after wandering for a long while through underground faults and cracks without a compass. I would never have suspected I was anywhere near where I came in. And now I looked round, the whole area seemed to have been converted. Alcoves had appeared in it, alcoves containing a grandfather clock (not going) and an imposing carved chair that might have been some eisteddfod or ceremonial chair. Very upright, very fierce, it dared anyone to feel worthy of it, but it had a forlorn look about it too, and was obviously dying to be sat in. I supposed they were pieces rescued from a gutted mansion, or things that had gone for a song at auction after the decease of the last descendant. Beautiful things, useless now: solid, intricate − quite out of place in the smooth, wide sweep of the foyer.

Only by the revolving doors and the now unoccupied desk did I know where I was, and I thought: there's probably some con-man chasing round, hastily fixing up revolving doors and desks wherever I go, to delude me into madness on top of everything else.

I wandered away from there, down other corridors, with a growing confidence that I had the place to myself. The dining-room, therefore, came as a surprise. I stood on the threshold, bewildered as if I had stumbled upon some secret organisation, feeling half inclined to tiptoe softly backwards and dissolve. A large family-party sat there, in the middle of the room, busy, the mainstream of life, wielding heavy, bulbous hotel cutlery that twanged dully as swords when the children, distracted by my appearance, let them collide. On the periphery, like satellites, smaller tables held couples, leaning in or leaning out, as if in spinning counterbalance; all, it seemed, posing in attidues of conspiracy. But I could make nothing of what they were all saying: their voices were soaked up by the carpet long before it reached my feet, bearing, as in homage, its golden oakleaves. They billowed like the feathers on some coat of arms. Even the walls looked cushioned, with red shapes standing out like the satin hearts on Valentine cards that come in handy as pincushions later on. Plush, I suppose, was the word. A puffy-looking room. Stuffed. Swollen.

Three people, I noticed, were sitting on their own. Maybe, after

6

all, it would be alright here. Say for a week anyway. I sat down at a small table just inside the door, in a draught.

The wallpaper revealed a propensity to cling, like Velcro.

'*Gaf i ymuno â ti?*'

I had my chin down while unsnagging my hair, so it was quite an effort to turn sideways to see who was being addressed.

'Pardon?'

'Mind if I join you?'

'No, no – you can sit where you like. Free country.'

'Sure? You look as if you might mind.'

'Why on earth should I mind?' It was insufferable the way young men found it impossible to tolerate indifference in a woman.

'You're not expecting anyone?'

'I expect nothing. Except to be left alone by this blessed wall.'

His arm swept in a gracious, complimentary arc over the table-cloth, revealing that his sleeves were too short. 'It's your irresistible magnetism.' I let that go: my hair, becoming rather matted, was requiring concentration. 'Here – let me release you from your hang-ups.'

I glared then. Things might have come to a pretty pass, but we were having none of that.

He was, however, falling over himself in his attempt at chivalry.

'Would you like to change places?'

The assumption of his own immunity from the wall's tentacles infuriated me. 'Thank you, but I suspect you're in an even bigger draught there than I am here. Also, the door's going to bang into you every time it opens.' He looked so naively disconcerted for a moment, that I added, in a kind of jovial gloom: 'The doors in this place are as unpredictable as the walls.'

He looked baffled – he was not, after all, a man to be trifled with by doors and walls. He was a man who would strike out confidently for the far shores of the seventh sea – it was what he was built for, with his aquiline nose and his heavily hooded eyes that didn't open very far. He seemed, moreover, all greased up ready for the job, black hair wetly tacky, face gleaming, waxed clothes, and greasy hands tapping the yellow tablecloth. Did the hotel have a swimming-pool, I enquired.

7

'Not unless you count the yard.'

'Where all the scaffolding is?'

'What? Oh, that's the fire-escape. If there's a fire, you choose between going up in flames and drowning.'

'Or applying the water to the flames.'

'Huh. You don't try to save this dump, you run. If you can't fly, that is.'

'I see.' But I was hardly in any position to take a severe line; a cornered mouse had nothing on the running I was doing. . .

He mistook my grimness. 'Sorry to worry you if you're staying here,' he said, leaning forward to rest his elbows on the table and toy with the salt. Clean nails tipped his greasy hands: neatly filed, very pink nails, healthy, young.

The door opened and shuddered at the contact with his chair. He spoke with friendly tolerance to the old man who had entered, tapping a white stick before him. But the old man did not reply.

'Shit,' he said. 'What are all these crazy doors doing here anyway?'

'It could prove vital to have more than one door to a place.'

'If there's a fire you can always break a window.'

'Not just in a fire.'

'When then?'

'Well.' He was annoying me, I was annoying him, and time was too short for such stupidity. 'When a cow comes in, for instance.'

'You mean a cow cow?'

'Yes.'

'Why the hell should a cow come in?'

'Lonely – they get lonely, too. Or it might just feel like coming in, on the spur of the moment.'

'In that case, the less fucking doors the better.'

'You wouldn't say that if you'd ever had to back a cow down a narrow hall.' I sounded as though I had spent my entire life shunting cattle down one-exit hallways.

My order came then, but I wouldn't let him get away with his muttered response. 'Don't be silly – how can you turn a cow round in a hall?' But he was placing his own order with the waitress. She obviously knew him, though she was resilient to the banter he tried to keep up with her (to prove how cantankerous was I, how charming was he). No doubt she had cynically watched him chat up woman after woman, and I kept my head down, not to give her the satisfaction of seeing how old I was.

'You were brought up in the country then?' he resumed.

'Was I?'

'I just thought, being such an expert on the bad habits of cows.'

'It's common knowledge that no animal likes reversing.'

'Doesn't it?'

'You seem to know the waitress quite well.'

'I'm from round here. You're not though, are you? Not a woman of your experience. You don't get cows in houses up this way. Cows know their place round here.'

It was only the men that didn't was it? But I kept quiet. He had lost his immaturely assured air and was looking bored and glum, and trapped in an ordinary sort of way. And after all, I should have said straight out at the start that I wanted to be alone. This was hardly the way to set about asserting myself against the world.

'Where is she anyway? And where's my steak? Didn't it ever cross your mind you might want to catch that cow in the hall, not let it out? What's that fish like?'

'Well, if a cow gets in here you'll catch it easily enough. Nothing, but nothing, would persuade it to negotiate those revolving doors in reverse. God knows it's hard enough getting round them when you're human and advancing.' The greased youth would sidle smoothly through, of course, without so much as brushing the doors, never mind stubbing his toe and then getting stabbed in the back. 'The fish is rather tasteless, thank you.'

'Do you want me to call Alice?' He revealed he was Douglas, by the way.

'I'll call her myself if I need her, thank you.'

'I just thought, seeing as I know her.'

'A kind thought.'

Years ago he would have been a teddy-boy. Did they still manufacture Brylcream for them, I wondered, now they were bald? It must be a long time since the market for washboards had collapsed.

'What's the matter now?' he asked when I peeped under the table.

'Nothing. I just wondered what shoes you were wearing.'

'Well for Christ's sake don't – you'll be getting yourself tangled up in the tablecloth next.'

He glanced around, rather discreetly for him. For a moment I thought he was going to smoke, but there was already an ashtray between us. So I took it that he was sizing up the talent – something he should properly have done before inflicting himself on me.

'I don't suppose I'd be the first – there's someone who looks as if he went through the wash with it.' I nodded at the man who had received me at the desk; he was wandering around the room with a distracting nonchalance, chatting to the diners, absently setting straight the cutlery at empty tables. He looked jaundiced, but perhaps his skin was simply reflecting the tablecloths.

'You mean his eyes popped when he surfaced? He's the manager you know.'

'Is he?' We were the only table not to be graced by a visit, but we had come in for more than our fair share of glances. My earlier self-denial of late-night encounters with the outside world, in refusing a key, had clearly lost its innocence: I was openly, unashamedly exploiting internal resources. I would leave in the morning. I celebrated the decision by drinking the wine that seemed to have appeared; red wine. 'He's certainly missing nothing. If his eyes pop any more, we'll have them rolling on the floor.'

'You know nothing about eyes rolling around the floor.'

'Do you?'

'Yeh – I used to share a flat with a bugger with a glass eye.'

'Goodness.'

'He kept arguing – just so's he could take it out and chuck it at you. Oh thanks – at last.' The sight of the bleeding meat seemed to loosen his tongue. 'He smashed up everything in that flat – you've no idea. It went through things like a cannon ball – bottles, glasses, the lot. He bust somebody's pinkie finger with it once, too. Got lethal when he was pissed. No aim, mind. Lost the damn thing every time. He'd have us crawling all over after it.' He up-ended the wine bottle over his steak until it was swimming. 'Everything you did, he bloody argued about. And everything you said.'

'Just as well I've no moveable parts then isn't it?' I allowed drily.

He looked up in surprise, and grinned.

'He can't get up to any of them tricks any more neither,' he remarked with satisfaction. 'He's had it whipped off him.'

'Heavens – who'd want to steal a glass eye?'

'No, no – he's in prison like, so they confiscated it.' He shrugged. 'Dangerous weapon, I suppose – and right too. He gets out in a month.'

'It'll be back sharing with him then, will it?'

'Not fucking likely.'

'He must look gruesome without the eye.'

'He wears a patch, someone said. I haven't been up.'

'No, I meant when he. . . used to take it out.'

'Oh. Dunno. Too pissed to notice. Yeh, I guess he is gruesome a bit. You get used to him though.' He sounded suddenly affectionate.

'What's he going to do when he's released?'

'Take his eye out and beg, I spect. He'll get by.' He chuckled. 'That socket's going to get so loose he'll need bigger and bigger eyes to stay in.' With embarrassing childishness he pulled the lid back from one of his own eyes and screwed up the other, greatly relishing the prospect.

It was raining in earnest now, driving at the glass with a kind of spite. Out in the roadway cars crawled by, already lit up, and sizzling as though they were red-hot metal searing the wet tarmac. Clouds of fumes bulged lazily in their wake and thinned out into nothing.

The comfortable room felt suddenly vulnerable. There was nothing there to offer any kind of resistance to anything. Nothing solid. Nothing supporting the upholstery. Nothing behind all the padding but hollow stud walls. It was as flaccid as the flesh of a face which has no bone structure to hold it up.

Soft. But what a scaring kind of comfort softness was.

I would leave first thing in the morning.

'You're making heavy weather of that fish.' Douglas sounded critical. His own plate was empty.

'Think I'll leave it at that. Excuse me a moment.'

But when I checked, the face in the mirror was as usual. Pain was evidently no guide to the way things looked. No hole was ever better concealed than the hole in my mouth. Douglas had been impatient merely, not astute. I felt how pathetic my relief was.

Of course I appeared normal. Look how the dentist had reacted, after all. Just yesterday. Greeting me with warmly welcoming surprise among the instruments. 'You're looking well. And how. . . what a tremendous job they've done.' Something like that. Yesterday. Exuding such heartiness – the heartiness of a man who had failed to diagnose a tumour until he burst it – blundering on and on. 'It's amazing what they can do these days you know – quite amazing. A very delicate operation, that. I confess I didn't think you'd get away without considerable disfigurement. How are you feeling?' Ironically, it was his own face that had altered then – I watched closely, and it altered. I suppose I must have been telling him I hadn't had the operation yet. He found it necessary to bend very low to wash his hands.

But then, as Douglas said, you get kind of used to gruesome faces.

And one advantage would be not being joined for meals by men like Douglas.

It was curious, the way young men were so objectionable. It made no difference whether they were eating steak in leather jackets on humid summer evenings, or welcoming you into their air-conditioned surgeries; they still took things for granted about you. It seemed to happen as soon as they began to lose their tentativeness towards you. But was that when you got to a certain age, or when they did?

The sad fissures running from either side of my nose to my chin by-passed the corners of my mouth, as though they were assiduously avoiding it. As well they might.

In the doorway of the dining-room, I was confounded by the same feeling of delusion I had had on unexpectedly coming across the entrance hall. There was no Douglas, and nothing on the table where we had been sitting. It had to be the wrong dining-room. Yet there was the manager, standing like a run-down mechanism now, gazing out of the window, or into the reflections there in the almost twilight. The only effects the con-man had been switching this time were the evidence of my passing. It was as ludicrous to think of sitting down for the next course as if twenty years had elapsed. My existence was clearly no longer continuous.

I went over to the waitress; she was slapping at crumbs with a tea-towel, making them jump, and looking as vicious as if she was swatting flies.

'May I have the bill please?' I half expected her to stare blankly, as at a face she had never before set eyes on.

'Oh, it's been charged to your account, madam.'

'Oh. Can I. . . could I just see the amount please?'

She sauntered cheekily away, high heels dangerous in this plummy world.

Despite the impossible toughness of bread, I might have to stick to snacks in future.

By the time I unfolded the transparent sliver of paper I was so self-conscious, balancing on the swell of oak-leaves, that the figures took a few seconds to register. When they did, however, I lost all sense of the public.

'Oh but – excuse me. Excuse me please. It shouldn't. . . I don't think it should be this much. You see, I'm only paying for the fish.'

'Excuse me,' the girl called down the room to the manager in a shrill voice sing-song with boredom. 'Come 'ere a minute, will you?'

He came over quickly enough: a few tables were still occupied.

'Madam 'ere says she's only paying for the fish, but the gentleman did say as she was paying for the lot.'

'Alright, Alice. Thank you.'

Alice hovered before reluctantly retreating. 'You could see it coming a mile off,' she muttered as she turned to cock her behind at the swing doors.

'Thank you Alice. Now. . . Miss Thomas. . .'

'Er. . . I'm afraid there's been some mistake. . .' I watched his lips move as he totted up the figures. 'No, it's not the arithmetic, it's the food – I didn't eat all that.'

'The food was eaten, madam.'

'Yes, there's been a lot of food eaten here tonight, but I'm not paying for all of it.'

'But sir apparently intimated. . .'

The whole messy year I had just lived through rose suddenly in a blur of red – red bills, red bank statements, red demands, red lines to be signed and counter-signed, selling everything, promising to pay everyone – and I didn't hear the rest of the sentence.

'Oh, sir apparently intimated, did sir? And I suppose that if sir were to apparently intimate that he wished to see the place burn to the ground around you, you would oblige sir with a box of matches? Well, sir has had his intimations. I am now having mine. I am not paying this bill.'

'The bill has to be paid madam.' He was cool and resolute, as with a child in a tantrum.

'I suggest you intimate that to sir. . .'

'I did wonder, madam. . . but. . .'

The unexpected flicker of sympathy was worse than the unjust insistence.

'Wonder? What's the good of wondering? If you stopped poking and prying and prowling, and did something instead. . .'

'Madam talks as if it was I cheated her.' He was aggrieved now.

'No. . . no. . . I'm not saying that. . .' The conversation had developed a limp. 'It's just that anyone could intimate anything, couldn't they?'

'But sir and madam were eating together,' he protested.

'Well, at the same table, perhaps. . .'

'And sharing a bottle of wine.'

I felt suddenly exposed, very publically exposed, and lapsed into an unhappy mutter. 'Well, I wouldn't have mentioned it normally. Normally I'd just have paid. . . But. . . It's just that. . . with things as they are. . .'

'I will bear it in mind that in future madam wishes to pay only for her own meals.' His gracious dismissive little bow was silly, silly.

I don't remember leaving the room. All I remember is being lost in the interminable passages again, exasperated with the world, disgusted with myself, and not even really trying or wanting to find my room. Then, in a slight recess, I noticed a hole in the wall, neat, round, six inches or so across, and two or three feet above the ground. The perfect 'o' of a mouth stretched in pain or ecstasy or the panic of death. A little further along there was another. Then none for a while, and then another. They might occur haphazardly, but they were always of the same size and at the same height. The walls were breathing – breathing or spying or listening, and these were the ducts that served as mouth and nose and eyes and ears.

I crouched down, but could see nothing. I stuck my fingers in: nothing. My hand in: space. A draught. My hand nosed down-wards, till I was up to the elbow in nothingness, then to the shoulder. My fingers must be groping close to floor level now. The tip of my longest finger swept past something – something warm and furry – I grazed the whole length of my arm tugging it out.

They were holes in a cardboard box letting the monster cooped up inside breathe. Or ventilation for secret, rat-infested passages.

Couldn't be. The ventilation grilles were high in the walls, close to the ceiling. Those looked normal enough anyway. Or did they? In several of them rolls of brown paper were caught – like secret messages left there long ago and never collected. Brown with age, or brown from the smoke of a fire that had curled them crisp and unintelligible.

They could almost be half-smoked cigars, resting there until the giant chose to pass that way again.

But when I fished a chair out of one of the bathrooms, I found that all they were were old rolled-up leaves stuck between the bars – though where autumn leaves came from in the middle of August and how they got wedged up there, remained a mystery.

The holes, I could not explain at all.

When eventually I came across my room, I pulled the bed away from the wall, but not expecting, never really expecting, behind it, the small familiar black hole that stared blankly back at me.

'Oh God.'

Well, there must be some reason for them. Or have been some reason once. Maybe there was an archaic central heating system in the place, that blew hot air out of the holes. But what was capable of blasting hot air at you, was capable of blasting everything else imaginable at you too – poison, nerve gas, anything. It was probably the building's defence mechanism against invaders.

I sat on the bed, unable to distract myself any longer from thinking about how I had lost my head in front of everyone – the hotel staff, other guests, everyone. Dignity might have been the last thing to go, but it had certainly gone now.

It was a bitter thing – to have clung to it so grimly in the face of the sympathy of relatives and the advice of neighbours and the embarrassment of friends, such as they were, only to lose it so fecklessly before a crowd of strangers.

To my disgust, and with relief, I came to cry, in the hard, obstinate way which seemed the only way of crying left. Painful, dry-eyed crying that only stopped when I felt the ugliness of my raucous breathing.

But when I raised my forehead from the cold, narrow rim of the white basin, all I could think was: however false and cloying all that plushness is downstairs, there is no comfort whatsoever up here.

I looked round the walls, stark shining walls with hooks on them, as though waiting for the sides of bacon to be strung up. I looked at the clean, plastic-looking curtains, hygienic as mortuary polythene. And through the windows, to where, should I ever try to get beyond them, the nailed planks would box me in like a coffin.

Any sort of comfort was better than none.

CHAPTER TWO

I came to in the pitch black, with no sense of being anyone or being anywhere. Just enjoying a sensation of motion, and enjoying the little mesmerising tinkles and trickles of water playing in some fragile fairyland. Until there intruded a brutally overbearing need to find out which way I was facing, in relation to whatever else there was. Fatal. The split second the outline of the window jumped onto the end of the bed, knowledge came like a fall.

It was no fun at all, this waking up with amnesia and un-intelligible misgivings, and having them give way to something like morning sickness as they became intelligible.

I turned to face the wall, heaving myself over like some odd, crusty creature that has spent a million years adapting itself to its environment, only to find it softens into susceptible flabbiness again the minute it stops struggling. Overnight.

There had to be some way of living in a trance, if I could only hit upon it.

The rills of fairyland suddenly took a distinctly tinny turn and became rather insistent and not at all fragile. The hotel's plumbing seemed to leave a lot to be desired. Either that, or the other guests did. I groped for the cord to the light above my bed, a striplight that flickered with insect-like ticking two, three times before asserting its harsh glare. Twenty past one. Much earlier than I thought. People couldn't be having wholesale baths at this hour, surely. The dribbles and gurgles high in the wall didn't seem inclined to cease. The whole system must be riddled with air-locks.

Occasionally there was a splurge, as from some overflow, splattering down into the yard like slops.

I would definitely leave in the morning.

17

Meanwhile, as anyone able to sleep through that racket would obviously sleep through anything, I toyed with the idea of having a bath myself.

I got as far as collecting the soap, in fact, before it struck me that the noises could well be outside. Now I was upright, they sounded positively outside. I went to the window. Noah, facing the world from the ark, in the aftermath of the downpour but with the floodwaters continuing to rise, must have felt similarly beleaguered. It was raining still, but unnaturally slowly and ponderously, and not from the sky. The mazes of waterlogged wooden decks oozed and dripped, from level to level, in a series of steps, down into the waterlogged yard. And all the noise came from the water gushing along the roof guttering, and gargling and spluttering as it hit the downpipes, and then sloshing down them. Now and again, when the drainpipes choked, they vomited into the pit below.

I closed the window and went back to bed. The sounds outside, subdued again now, were astonishingly like language – like garbled rumours spreading about the destruction of the world. And spreading they were, with a vengeance – a panic-struck depraved glugging started up in the wastepipe from my basin. I stifled that with the plug, but then had to release it to take some pills, which I reckoned were the only way I was going to get any more sleep.

I lay face down with the pillows over my head, but it was like an orchestra tuning up out there now – an orchestra ranged round the tiers of balconies which had the acoustics of an amphitheatre. When some urgent chattering started up close at hand, I tried to think of it as a jay scolding me to sleep, but I had just noticed my long-forgotten rings on its horny ankle when it was interrupted by a magnificent prima donna swoosh, gloriously denying all it had said, but ending badly in a few cynical hiccups.

I threw the pillows on the floor (they were suffocating me anyway), got out of bed, turned the taps on full, and got back into bed. Now I had to contend not only with an increased volume of sound but also with fears about an intrusive volume of water that could easily get out of hand. I got up, turned the taps off, picked

18

up the pillows from the floor, and flung them out the window, sending them scudding over the fire-escape and down into the flood in the yard, and went back to bed.

The clamour did seem to be subsiding a bit, and I willed myself to be lulled by the soft lapping and sucking, trying to get my mind fixed less on a waterfall and more on a lake. But it was probably the pills that sent me into the semi-comatose state I was in when there was an outburst of maniacal bubbling laughter. I sat up in drugged fury. We had advanced from the ark, it appeared, to the Tower of Babel.

Soothing murmurs arose, patronising me, and then they too grew still. And all that broke the silence after that was the occasional tap-tapping of lonely, esoteric questioning and the odd exasperated plop it provoked in reply.

I dreamed I wanted to speak but I had no mouth. They had to cut one into me, but they made a hash of it, so that when I tried to talk it was painful and the sounds that came from it were unintelligible. This, they said, could be cured by teeth, which they set about hammering into the hole they had made in my face.

Hammering. My mind must have gone back to air-locks, because my first thought on coming round was: Christ, we've got pipe-hammer now on top of everything. I had read an article once on how to cope with pipe-hammer: the quirky style came back vividly, but what the devil had it said?

I sat up and the hammering leapt outside and I remembered the pillows. What on earth had I gone and done that for? I had to get them back: quick. It would soon be getting light. The milkman would see them floating around. Or would they have sunk by now? I didn't much fancy the idea of wading out for them (having to swim for them?), nor of groping down all those pitch-black passages with their draughts and eerie holes, getting lost. . .

And if I did fish them out, I would somehow have to surreptitiously dry out half a ton of sodden feathers or explain to someone that my pillows fell out of the window.

Surely I could just take others from some cupboard (what cupboard?) or some spare room and no-one would be any the wiser?

It was something I would never have contemplated countenancing in the most uncontrollable child when I'd been deputy head.

Well, when God gives you a tumour, he must expect the consequences.

The hammering was getting feverish: it sounded as though a whole team of hammerers were working against the clock. Erecting another platform, no doubt – and as frantic about it as if they built the scaffold for a hanging at daybreak. The blows were falling faster than my pulse – much faster, and drawing closer. I imagined the web of platforms hammered tighter and tighter, drawn like a brace around the building, throttling it.

How silly. It wasn't hammering at all, it was footsteps. Stealthy feet running along those wooden alleyways. A regiment pounding along the duckboards of some front-line trench. You could imagine the bodies belonging to those feet bent double, fearful of being seen above the parapet. If there were any bodies to them, that was.

This really was the limit. The whole place was haunted. I would go – first thing in the morning, I would go. And with all the dissatisfaction of having made up my mind for the tenth time, I humped the blankets over my head.

But even under there the sounds reached me – subhuman scamperings now, like the scuttling of rats on a doomed ship. Rats scurrying to and fro along the railings: frenetic activity to stall the decision to jump for it. As if they knew only the sea lay below the frail decks. Then, silence.

I stuck my head out – there was a conspiratorial murmuring of voices that was entirely human.

It was no good – I would have to get up and find out what was going on.

Half-past two. What a night! I turned the light off again before going to the window, and grazed my shin on the corner of the bed.

It came as a surprise to find real people out there – people making the boards creak above my head, and moving along the top level of the fire-escape opposite. I saw only shadows, but they were the substantial shadows of starlight, not the insubstantial shadows of the sun. They were neither running nor talking now – just creeping around. What could they be doing, the legs that flickered between the slats above me, jerking like dancers under strobe lighting, and the heads across the yard from me? They seemed at odds, legs going one way, heads another, like decapitated fowl. Could they be other guests who had forgotten their keys and were sneaking in up these back staircases and corridors? Or illicit guests, perhaps, not entitled to keys, but needing, like everyone else, somewhere to spend the night?

What I ought to have done, instead of coming to a strange hotel to brood and wait alone, was get involved in something active that needed a quick, one-track mind and left no time to stop and think.

They were dragging things now, heavy things – heaving them along the boards.

There was a lull, and then a light – a torch-beam uncertainly advancing through a doorway in the far corner of the yard. I tiptoed out and leaned over the wooden rail, straining to see whether it would pick out my pillows. A clatter made me jump. Before I realised it was a dustbin lid I saw a black movement; something leaping out of the bin, a cat or a rat, I couldn't tell which from the second floor.

The pinpoint of brightness swung into view. The footsteps behind it were unlike the others – a sharp, metallic, robot-like tread on a mat of scrapers. And the ray of light that swung round the yard seemed charged: it started up movement wherever it shone. It was as though the beam lured the very water from the flood, sucking it up into the air and letting it fall back, as from too weak a magnet.

There couldn't be fish down there, surely? (Of my pillows, I was relieved to notice, there was no sign.)

Frogs – they were frogs of course, a veritable plague of frogs. Probed into action by the light as surely as if they were wired up in some laboratory and subjected to electric shocks. When the beam retreated indoors, everything relaxed, and I went back in.

As soon as I was in bed, the whole scene outside felt unreal – like a set piece played out by mechanised toys that had now run down.

The only other thing I heard that night was the siren of a police-car.

At breakfast, the manager was the only person in evidence. He crossed the golden oakleaves looking morose and tired, aggrieved I was up so early perhaps.

'I'll let the girls know you are here.'

'Thank you.'

'I hope you had a comfortable night.'

'A lot of people seemed to come in very late.'

'Oh? Did they? I hope they didn't disturb you.'

'Didn't they disturb you?'

'No.'

'I thought I saw you looking around the yard with a torch.'

'Oh. Oh, is that what the noise was? Yes, I thought I heard something and went out to look.' He flicked at a tablecloth where neither dust, nor flies, nor crumbs had settled. 'Some people use the fire-escape, you know, because it's more convenient.'

'I just wonder how good it would be in a fire.'

He stooped to lean on his fists on my table. For a second I thought he was going to whisk the tablecloth from under my elbows, but if the thought had crossed his mind, concern for his crockery prevailed.

'Why's that?'

'Well, with it being wood.'

He surveyed me intently, as though he suspected that what he had heard in the middle of the night had been me ejecting my greasy young companion of last evening onto the fire-escape.

'If there are flames tearing through a fire-escape you don't use it whatever it's made of, do you?' He drew himself slowly upright and flexed his shoulders as though he had backache, adding offhandedly: 'And if there aren't flames tearing through it, what's wrong with wood?'

It didn't seem the right moment to mention I was leaving after breakfast.

'It has been treated, of course,' he remarked as he left, apparently implying I should be too.

When I'd been served, he became affable. 'Muggy as ever

22

despite all the rain in the night, isn't it? Have you got anything interesting planned for today?'

It might have been an excellent opening, but the sausage I was chewing was hot. 'Well as a matter of fact. . . I was thinking. . . that perhaps I ought to. . . seeing as the weather. . .' The protruding eyes seemed to penetrate to the back of my skull. Oh what the hell anyway? What was the good of chasing miserably from place to place? 'Thought I might go for a walk.' Well, why not? I hadn't given the communing with nature tack a try yet. 'Explore around a bit.' He had instinctively glanced at the windows and was looking doubtful. 'Are there any walks round here you could recommend?'

'Well, there's the river, I suppose.' He sounded even more doubtful than he looked. 'But they're poisoning the rats down there.'

I went nevertheless.

To avoid meeting him again, I left by the fire-escape. In the daylight it looked a crazy enough affair, but then I suppose there was no alternative given the hotel's hotch-potch of styles. Devising the thing at all must have been something of a nightmare, particularly on the Victorian block where I was: and in the end a few higgledy windows, which appeared to be on a stairwell I had not discovered, had got overlooked and been by-passed, and little off-shoots had to be sent back, or up, or down, to collect them. It had obviously been easier to design on the two parallel modern blocks of the square, where the windows were at least regular, but even there, because of the slope, the roofs and windows were stepped, and so the escape had to be stepped too. On the fourth side of the square, though, along the back of the huge old farmhouse, the escape was simply a mess: so haphazard were the windows it was like crazy-paving all over the wall, and spilt over onto the roof, even, where there were skylights. On the whole, it was a construction you began by deploring and ended by marvelling at. I could detect no orifice that had escaped its clutches, bar two tiny windows high in the farmhouse – gauged to be too small, I suppose, for a human being to squeeze through even in the direst extremity.

The boards were still slippery after the rain, dangerous even. There were patches shining with slime, and patches covered in livid green fungus, and the whole lot was so sodden it looked as if it would be less likely to catch fire than put it out.

The yard lay underneath me like a moat, which seemed a shame when the drainage system displayed across the facades was as elaborate as the fire-escape system with which it was entangled. Under horizontal troughs, drainpipes were rakishly angled down the walls like traditional caravan chimneys, to circumvent obstacles, in what could have been taken for a model of some ingenious, ancient irrigation system. But beneath the fine network of capillaries, the main vein was clearly blocked. The mountains might have been sucked meticulously dry, but the estuary was silted up.

I tried to wade blindly through, but there was a pillow. It had fetched up against the dustbin jetty and had developed a problem I had not anticipated: mud. I ignored it, but then felt so guilty about all the people it would interfere with – butchers lugging carcases into the kitchen, or dustmen bearing the stripped bones away – that I went back and crammed it into one of the dusbins and put a stone on top of the lid.

Around my feet, petals were floating, translucent petals that had been there a long while. Somewhere else they had been blossom, but they had come drifting down here and got trapped. They had turned a pale brown at the edges and along their creases and tears, but some exuded still a faint flush of pink.

I went under the arch of the tradesman's entrance out into the lane – that was flooded too, but with water so brackish it seemed to absorb all reflections. It was a far cry here from the recognised entrance to the hotel – from the revolving glass doors in which all the overlapping reflections were disconcerting as images in a goldfish bowl.

From the back road you would never have guessed that the farmhouse was part of the same hotel. It looked so deserted I risked trying what had once been the front door, but it seemed stuck, glued to its frame by the pitch that coated it perhaps, and the seaweed slung over the horseshoe nailed there disintegrated in my hand, wet as it was. It might have been a derelict building but for the board nailed above a basement door at the end of a flight of worn stone steps under the road. The large, daring letters of *The Hungry Cheese* leapt in an angry flash of red at the feet of passing motorists.

It felt surprisingly rural there. The outbuildings across the road from the farm backed onto fields which sloped down to the river, its course marked way into the distance by the meandering lines of hawthorn scrub. There was no sign, however, of the Abbey ruins I half-expected to see (its monastery had been supplied by the original farm on the site where I was standing), so I wandered downstream where I figured they might be.

The river was swollen, and full of the debris of twigs and leaves it had torn from trees. It seemed the boundary to the farmland, and to the summer. For up from the opposite bank empty tracts of moorland covered with bog-cotton stretched to a horizon that looked snow-covered. But that was how this summer was: a summer that had grown tired of itself and sunk into a humid depression, and teased of winter.

It kept up appearances, of course, with new growth spurting everywhere in the wet warmth. But even there along the river-bank you could see what a heady kind of growth it was: delve anywhere into the lush undergrowth and you found a hot, moist festering where only fungi thrived. The summer was rotten to the core.

There was no sun, but I was covered with a film of sweat and I lay down on a dryish hummock, losing heart for the Abbey ruins. The sky glowered at me through the branches of an ash that not even such a summer as this could prise into leaf. How bleak a thing it was, to die. I cupped my head in the pillow of my palms and watched the rise and fall of my breathing. How was it possible that so much blood and bone and muscle could be lifted, and suspended on a pocket of air, and lowered again, without any sensation of strain at all?

So easily, just that easily, must a tumour grow, bulging like lungs, shoving up the bone and blood and muscle, with no effort and no pain. Stretching in you, little by little, as you move, and

25

laugh, and chew. Stretching while you are asleep. And nothing you can do, and nowhere you can go, will release you from it. And finally, insidiously, the symptoms appear.

The first twinge, of course, is nothing – one of those hardly noticeable twinges everyone keeps getting in all sorts of odd places for absolutely no reason at all.

The ruins turned out to be a disappointment. All the surprise I had on finding them, concealed in a low clearing behind a sparsely wooded bank, quickly died away. The grasses grew as tall as the crumbled walls: even the broad carved columns could not rear clear of the vegetation. Cow-parsley seeds drifted across the tops of them and floated away towards a lake choked with a mesh of bulbous stems, like a tangle of struggling arms drowning there. Only the odd lily had surfaced, its tight painted lips pouting fiercely as any stone angel's.

It had been, once, a massive place. The walls were thick and enclosed a vast area of nettles and thistles. It was trees that had done for them – old lichen-covered oaks, pitifully stooped to the wind and far too feeble any longer to turn even the stones of the field. But they had burst open the Abbey and flourished as its portals and lintels had tumbled around them. Then they had aged. The wizened trunks bore worse signs of ravage now than the sculptured stones they had ousted.

On one oak, at the altar end, there was a splash of red, dark like clotting blood. I went over to it. The trunk looked as if it had been burnt, and the bare earth around it was fine, as though mingled with soot. Nailed to the bark, as to a cross, was a wreath of red roses.

'*Hei, beth ar y ddaear wyt ti 'n wneud?*'

I turned round and saw below me, not visible from any but this wall of the Abbey, two caravans, tucked in closely under the bank, like children lurking and spying. In front of them, a scarecrow was staring up at me.

'Pardon?' I had hardly touched the wreath – and I had only wanted to find out whether the flowers were real in any case.

'It's private property here. Shove off.'

The young man was very thin, with dishevelled flaxen hair that petered out rather wispily on his shoulders. His jeans were faded and holiday-ish, but it seemed an odd way for tourists to behave.

'I'm only looking at the Abbey. I'm not interested in your ugly caravans.'

'You're trespassing. Piss off.'

But I didn't move. I was distracted by something working its way up through the grass towards me. A snake? But it was a rat; a rat battling up the slope as though it dragged behind it the sack of its own body. Sick. Paralysed. I was reminded of the noise I had heard along the slats of the fire-escape during the night, that slow inexorable shush of sacks being hauled.

A sharper movement recalled me. The man, quick as though he had flinched, had stooped for a stone.

'Are you going?'

'Do you really think I'm likely to vandalise your lousy vans?'

'I'm warning you.' His arm was moving back and up.

'Alright. But if you throw that I shall sue you.'

His laughing as I scrambled up the bank, too hastily, too easy a target, was low and bitter, and I didn't look back.

He belonged somehow to that oppressive summer, just as I did. His lank limbs, his long straggling hair made it seem he had grown with too little air or too little light. Behind the mane his face seemed like mine – on the point of caving in; his eyes were invisible already, either very deep-set or obscured by the shaggy eyebrows. But we were very different. I was outwardly sturdy and woody still, inwardly eaten away. But he was the spineless, uncontrolled growth that has never had any heart, it has grown so fast: the plant that outgrows its strength early, and straggles and goes to seed before it has matured. Different enough, certainly, but neither of us were of the stuff that would inherit the earth.

That was the way I remembered him.

CHAPTER THREE

'Oh, they'll be. . . er. . . distilling over there then, I expect. Something like that.' The manager became vague; he had begun by
unctuously reassuring me there were only tourists up at the
Abbey. 'There's plenty of it goes on. Nobody bothers about it
much.'

'Distilling?' It came out shrilly; I had a pang of guilt about all
the tap water I had topped up the car-battery with in the days
when I had been a car-owner. 'Distilling what?'

'Oh it'll be Welsh whisky, that.' He pursed his lips teasingly
under his mocking fishes' eyes.

'Oh.'

'Didn't know we had any of that now, did you?' He was
insinuating, not quite kind.

'No.'

'Caravans can be very deceptive.'

'Oh, I meant to ask you – where can I get a drink, please?'

'Do you mean, in the town?'

'Isn't there a bar in the hotel?'

'Yes, of course.' I caught his wary glance: drink had been added
to my list of shortcomings. 'You want to keep away from that
Abbey, you know,' he warned, as if he suspected the shortcoming
was about to be compounded by the illegal nature of the alcohol.

'Why?'

'Dangerous – those walls are dangerous – the whole place.'

The walls, waist-high at most, hadn't looked anything like as
dangerous as the man.

'There was a wreath there – pinned to a tree.'

'Wreath?'

'As though someone's just been buried there.'

'Buried? Oh no – they don't bury over there now. All the burials are up the valley, at Bont Ddu or Craigcefn.'

'What's the wreath doing there then? A red wreath.'

'Ah – poppies maybe. They might use the place as a war memorial.' He nodded once or twice, as if in approval of his suggestion.

But it was August, and they hadn't been poppies.

'Well, I think you should warn guests about the place before they go, not after they've been. I might have got stoned.'

'Pardon?'

'By a very thin, very aggressive man.'

'He wouldn't have hurt you.'

'Oh, you know him then do you?'

'No, no – I've seen him around that's all – from your description, like – I heard. . . someone like that was down there.'

'How can you possibly know he wouldn't have hurt me?'

'He's just a bit simple, that's all – you have to feel sorry for him, really.'

'Wait till he kills someone,' I said grimly. 'Or perhaps he already has, and buried them and bought the wreath out of remorse. Not,' I added even more grimly, 'that there was much evidence of remorse in his present mood.' Catching the look on his face, I found myself persisting, confidingly: 'I wouldn't be surprised if there wasn't some kind of black magic going on there, would you? After all, it is an oak grove, even if it's growing out of an Abbey.' I called after him: 'You can imagine them getting a special kick out of that, can't you?'

I didn't leave that day, and I didn't leave the next day either. Nor the day after that. I told myself it would look suspicious, and when that became obvious nonsense, I thought I would just stay to find out what was going on. Then I stayed, as one tends to stay, because lethargy sets in. And finally, there became another reason. And anyway, the waiting had to be got through somehow. So I ended up staying my allotted span.

The manager had neglected to tell me where the bar was. But it was something to go and look for, at least – and buildings didn't fluctuate like rivers and trees, to remind me of the growth in the bones of my face.

To tell the truth, the hostility of the man at the caravans had rather unnerved me. Anyone can do anything to you when you wander beyond the reach of walls and ceilings and doors.

So I nosed around the corridors, trying not to notice the turnings I took or the stairs I climbed, or the culs-de-sac I by-passed via the fire-escape. It meant it took me longer to turn up my room again, and it meant I could explore the same places time after time, scarcely recognising them. But your brain just won't be willed into ignorance and confusion: it tricks you by working things out in your sleep and you wake up to find you have made some sort of sense of wherever you happen to be staying.

The hotel did its best, however, to defy any sort of sense. One morning, in a part I had despaired of getting lost in, I came upon a huge, musty, windowless hall with microphones hanging awry as though they had been strangled and abandoned in a panic. In one corner several jackets had got left behind, flung among half-empty beer bottles and some smashed glass. One narrow tunnel led down to it from the fire-escape, and that was all. The mass of intersecting corridors that must have been snuggling round it like bloodvessels round a foetus, passed by oblivious. You could have spent your life in the building and never even suspected its existence, so subtly did all the changing levels and directions obscure the fact that there was an area not accounted for. I wondered how many other such rooms there were, rooms like dungeons suspended into the labyrinth by a thread from the airy, flimsy skywalks.

Oh, that's the hall we lease out,' the manager explained.

'It looks a bit. . . wrecked somehow.'

'Get the flashing lights going and the music blaring and the kids don't notice.'

'No, I suppose not.'

'Not worth putting new stuff in – those kids ruin everything.'

'Is that why it's sealed off from the rest of the hotel?'

'Well, the soundproofing was easier that way too.'

'Do you get much vandalism here?'

'You shouldn't go gallivanting all over the fire-escape, you know – it's not safe.'

Like the Abbey.

'Don't you think it should be? A fire-escape?'

'Well, don't blame me if you fall and break your neck.'

I wandered off morosely. 'You'll let me know if you turn up anything suspicious, won't you?' he called out mockingly.

Which is why I told him of the streaker I found in the attic.

I had left the attics till last, partly because they were least likely to contain the bar, I suppose, but also with some idea of saving the best bits to the end.

Curiously, they didn't have all the dead ends of the lower floors. There was the same warren of ways up there, but you did feel you were getting somewhere, laterally at least. What you lost, particularly in the old wings, was any feeling of contact with the floors below. And what contact there was, in my wing, was unpredictable. Steep spiralling steps, apt to deposit you in the middle of a room, had no doubt once given the servants frequent heart-failure, though they must have had an even bleaker time of it in the old farmhouse attics, where there were no stairs what-soever (and I could find no sign of trap-doors or loft-ladders either) – only connecting doors from the modern wings either side. The roof-space can't, in fact, have been designed for human habitation at all; it had shoulder-high walls and gaps instead of doors, that made you feel you were moving around stalls in a long-defunct cattle-market. But at the far end the walls had been badly extended to the roof-timbers and doors had been roughly fitted, as though some hermit had hung out there for a while.

I was standing puzzling at a glass bottle hanging on a level with my head when the apparition manifested itself in a doorway, quite close. Its mouth agape, as though seeing me had sent all thought clean out of its head.

It was a remarkable head. The shaved scalp on both sides was surmounted by a brilliant, if not luminous, rainbow crest running from forehead to crown. As the idea of it being the headgear of some elaborate costume was undermined by the nudity of the rest of his body, I could only conclude it must, either actually or notionally, be hair.

We reacted badly to each other. For a second he stood

31

transfixed, as the devil might, caught in an awkward moment during transmogrification to a turkey-cock. Then, misjudging my horror, he clasped his genitals and dissolved in reverse.

'You know you've got squatters, don't you?'

The manager contemplated me, drew himself to his full height and sighed. But I was adamant. 'In the old farmhouse.'

'Squatters.' He decided to accept it, but as fantasy rather than fate.

'Squatters. Definitely.'

'Er. . . how many. . . at a rough guess. . . would you say there were?'

'Well, one definitely.'

'Ah.'

'But judging from the noises, more.'

'Ah.' There was a pause before he asked, reluctantly: 'Noises?'

'Voices.'

'Ah. Saying what?'

'They were talking in Welsh.'

'Ah.' Once more he seemed to be making an effort to sound anxious. 'You didn't see any sign of their corporeal beings?'

'I saw one. Looking like the half-flayed cockerel of some disputed species.'

'Ah.' The tone was different – he knew him. And he saw I knew he knew him. 'That'll be Ceri Griff, I expect. At the machines again, was he?'

'I've no idea what he was at. He wasn't dressed for much.'

'Dressed?'

'No.'

'He's one of the Mohicans.'

'Yes, I had a suspicion he was extinct.'

'Where did you. . . run him to ground?'

'Up in the. . . oh, round about – I forget exactly. Well, in the attic actually.' I had suddenly seen an aspect to the encounter I had not considered.

'The attic in the old farmhouse?'

'Yes.'

'Your room is on the second floor of this wing.'

32

'Yes.'

'What were you doing up in the farmhouse attic?'

'I was just wondering what those old glass bauble things were, hanging up there.' I was burbling rather. 'With. . . purple liquid in them.' I hesitated to say methylated spirits. It might have been tactless (his 'Welsh whisky' could have been a euphemism for pretty well anything) or, given his likely opinion of me by now, he might have put the wrong interpretation on my interest in meths.

'They're for putting out fires.'

'Out?' I wasn't equal to his sense of humour.

'They contain ammonia.'

'Oh, I thought it was meths.'

'Ah.'

After scorn like that, I resolved to say nothing if I saw a gang of Mohicans tying bales of straw to the fire-escape.

The entire hotel seemed rigged up for a fire. It was obsessed by fire. Had there, perhaps, been a fire? That fantasy I'd had about the grandfather clock and bardic throne being salvaged from flames – was it half-registered charred scars that had given me that? It was worrying, with so many culs-de-sac around.

'What exactly are you supposed to do with those bottles of ammonia if there ever is a fire?'

'Get one in each hand and smash them together into the flames.'

'But they're glass.'

'Yes.'

'Oh. It must be the blood pouring from your lacerated wrists that puts out the fire, is it?'

'There are modern fire extinguishers on your floor.'

'Yes. I was just wondering, in case I lost my way in the smoke – or the heat of the moment.'

'Should you, in that event, fear for your wrists while fleeing for your life, you may take the bottles of ammonia by the neck and hurl them into the flames like hand grenades.'

'What about the fumes from the ammonia?'

'They waft up the chimney.'

'If the flames are in the fireplace, why put them out?'

'Just to be on the safe side, if I were you, I should douse any flames you come across.'

'He was starkers, you know, that Mohican,' I said, and walked away.

I never knew when he was teasing me and when he was coldly appraising me, that man, and even now, looking back to that first evening, I couldn't make out whether his prowling in the dining-room had been protective or accusing.

Douglas I had not set eyes on since. I talked to no-one at mealtimes now, and despite the hordes that regularly thronged in the dining room, the corridors were deserted still. All I ever saw on my floor were the traces of people who had just gone, the mist left on a mirror, the rim around the bath, and the slimy flat shampoo sachet on the basin, with the grizzled bit at the corner, where irritated jaws a sight stronger than mine, had chewed away at it. And all I heard were far-off taps running or toilets flushing, or, at night, scruttings out on the fire-escape. For the most part I absorbed these noises easily enough, much as you absorb real sounds in a dream. Only on bad nights, when nothing could get rid of the taste in my mouth and when I stared out between the bars like a mouse cornered in an orange-box, did I wonder how I could be sure I existed, now that nobody knew me.

The manager was the only person I ever spoke to.

By and large, though, I was finding, you don't need to com-municate much. People are pretty immune to each other most of the time, after all, even jam-packed in buses and tubes and on escalators: we all go through life, I suppose, more or less accidentally coming across an individual here and there we can relate to. There just happened to be no-one around any more on the same wavelength as me; that was all. It hardly mattered. I was in a world where jamming, and crossed wires, and lines rent in disturbances of one kind or another, were the order of the day. You groped around in the wreckage, and all you could find was some half-understood contact. But that would do, too.

And so I felt no particular need to speak to anyone except the manager.

They were wet days and wet nights. I grew tired of listening in the dark to the water spurting like gouts of blood from the gutters, and, when daylight broke, of seeing the whole empty day stretching ahead, and nothing but night again beyond that.

Yes, the nights were wet and the days were wet, but on the whole it was pleasant enough there, and I survived contentedly enough, one way and another. I would lean over my balcony and watch through the mornings the build-up of cloud high over the farmhouse chimneys: bulbous white cloud at first perhaps, then a soft dove-grey, then steel, sinking lower and lower, spreading out, flattening, and blotting out the three dimensions of the sky. And just as the chimneys began to lose their colour and recede, and you expected a downpour, there would topple out of the mist just one large drop, and then one more, marking the grey wood of the fire-escape and smarting there, like acid. Heavy drops, quickly stifled. The few hard tears pressed from eyes not accustomed to crying. Before the cloud passed on, self-contained again.

As long as I stayed in my cell, I was safe. Snug and dry. With my skull picked as clean as it had been in the X-rays, lit up on the screen, while the doctor's living, delicate finger had traced for me, with courtesy and care, the outline of where I had been eaten away. But behind the lucid wrist, the white cuff had been stern, and the white buttons, and the white lapels, and the head, that had spoken the one sentence and then gone on talking, but under the sea.

'Now, no-one likes having a tumour, but you shouldn't immediately assume it's sinister.'

He is God, and you know he is God because in one breath he has sucked your brain out of your skull like an egg out of its shell.

But you stare at your stripped bones, and you struggle.

Something not right. Something. Something desperately, urgently wrong. Not me – it wasn't me. It was a tiny old woman's head, narrow and pointed – some tiny old woman. The idiots had got the X-rays muddled, like one always heard – those damn idiots. . . please, dear God, please let them have got the X-rays muddled. Taken from crown to chin, one's head looks un-naturally elongated, the poised finger explains. Caught suddenly by the light, its moving flesh glows, pink like salmon.

You sit still, dry and safe in a bubble, while the whole world

35

dissolves, pounding around your ears. You have to sit very still, so as not to burst the bubble.

Students break through your deafness in a horrible parody of familiar classroom noise. The menacing syllables 'oma' jar, like the flat note on a schoolroom piano. They have trouble with their spellings, ameloblastoma, coronoid processes, neck of condyle, loculated periphery. They look up, look round, look down, everywhere but at your dummy's head, to which the words apply, and to which they are meaningless. But the chief of the gods squats eventually to look you straight in the eye and tell you not to fall over or bump into things or your face will crumple up: he mouths it clearly, letting you lip-read, for he seems to know that you are under the sea.

Oh yes, he is God, and you know he is God, but you stare at those stripped bones, and you don't half struggle.

It was long, long since. The starched overalls at my elbow had become calcified, under the dripping tap, into white vitreous china. The room had emptied. Through the walls came the deadman gurgle as the plug in some other basin was pulled.

It was like a brain itself, the hotel, cell upon cell upon cell. Threaded with nerves that reached out from the central areas towards the tiny, hidden, inaccessible parts, their impulses growing weaker and weaker. . .

I found the bar. It was the Hungry Cheese of course.

It was blissfully cool down there, the lunch-time I first went – cool and dark and deserted. I could see nothing at first as I crept through the unlatched door and across the massive flagstones. Then I made out coconut and reed matting and a threadbare Persian rug and the whitewashed walls, marked by green stains that showed which stones in them sweated. A single picture hung there – modern, a childish arrangement of red and black blotches.

I sat facing it on one of the settles set sideways to the huge open fireplace, with my knees against the rim of one of the old halved beer-barrels that had been made into tables. The brass fender was shining: behind it heavy black fire-irons, bent into gaunt arthritic shapes, hung over the fine ash of newly-burnt wood. So newly burnt I could still smell it. I felt like a child haunting the sad and awesome scene of abandoned merriment, stealing among the debris while the adults are tucked away, sleeping it off somewhere else. I was startled to hear a sound – of some dusky Indian servant, gliding across dried palm fronds.

It was the manager, his luminous eyes looking more as if they could see in the dark then ever.

He grinned at my surprise with ironic self-deprecation, inferring I had penetrated his other life and was now implicated in it too.

It came as less surprise, when I went back there that evening, to find the Mohican plucking darts out of the far wall. His reaction at seeing me was a surreptitious glance at the only other person in the bar, his opponent. It was Douglas.

'Oh, hello there.' He managed to look a bit put out; enough to make me sit down obstinately rather than retreat, but not enough, I gauged, to refund me for his meal.

'Hello.'

'Small world isn't it?' Since we were in the bar of the hotel where we had met a week previously, I was rather lost for words. 'Do you play?' He extended three wicked-looking spikes at me on his open palm.

'No, but I'll have a whisky please.'

He hurled his handful of darts like javelins at the board.

I jumped – the hinged section of the bar had crashed back into place – and the manager was with us. Or was he? He was advancing with both arms stretched out in front of him and his wide eyes glaring, like a man walking in his sleep. But he grabbed the shoulders of the Mohican and shook him, shouting at him in Welsh. The flamboyant quiff vibrated. Douglas made some attempt to intervene but was quelled with a look and a scathing comment in an undertone: the lad offered no resistance at all. When he was put down he pulled his clothes back into shape with no sign of self-consciousness or wounded pride or shame. His face, bearing none of the defiance his appearance suggested, was utterly passive. The hotelier's, however, darkened when he saw me.

'Martini?' he conjectured coldly.

'Douglas is very kindly buying me a Scotch,' I said firmly.

'Make that a double – alright?' came from Douglas.

'Oh, well, thank you.' I was more pathetic than the Mohican, who at least hadn't thanked the man that had abused him.

The manager came beside me to throw a log on the fire that was now lit. It was a tiny fire, and poor, for the wood was green and spluttered and spat as though fighting madly with the little life that was left in it still.

'You keep a fire here even in summer then?'

'Yes, in the evenings – the place is so damp everything gets mildewed if I don't.'

Every flame that appeared was reflected many times in the brass of the fender, and made the room seem ripe and lively, but it only lasted a moment or two. Most of the time, there was just a starry glow in a cave that the fire had eaten into the wood.

I watched the pair of them playing darts; but they seemed inhibited and left, and against the upright back of the settle I felt I was a prim and forbidding presence.

Some time later, locals from the town came in, shaking dripping plastic and wet hair, and apologising to me just as they were about to flop onto the settle, and withdrawing, not drying themselves off at the fire after all. So I left, then.

But I went back, and I came to know when it was likely to be crowded and when it wasn't and I avoided the popular times. Whatever time I went, the Mohican was likely to be there, but he was usually on his own, and I didn't mind being there with him then. He would crouch on top of a barstool like some moping, brooding cockatoo, as far away from me as he could get, and although I occasionally felt some impulse (redolent of my days as deputy head) to grab him by his three ear-rings and shave him completely so that he could start again from scratch, we never spoke or smiled or acknowledged each other's presence at all. He obviously had no job and no interests and nothing at all to do. Neither had I, of course, but that was beside the point. I was waiting for an operation.

He must have collected the dole on Tuesdays, because on the Tuesday he got drunk and from then until the end of the week he drank less and less, and at the weekend he cadged. It was always beer he drank. We probably each told ourselves we tolerated the other for the sake of the drink.

It was so quiet there sometimes, with just the two of us, that you could hear a faint crackling on the floor – a tiny, rather eerie sound, as though lice were dropping from the old beams strung across the ceiling. He was hearing it too, I could tell, for he would glance along the floor, puzzled, and then look above his head, as though he were likewise imagining the rotting beams teeming with life. But perhaps all we heard was the seep of water, ticking between the flagstones, or the stones themselves contracting, or the snapping jaws of the beetles that must live beneath them. I found it disturbing, for it reminded me of the faint crackle of little flames, like a field of stubble burning in the far distance.

And in the long noons at the empty hearth, with the fire in my throat to take the taste away, I turned over and over in my head the words that were branded there like a poem one has learnt too young. 'Now no-one likes having a tumour, but you shouldn't immediately assume it's sinister.' Sinister. Cancer. But weren't other things sinister too? Weren't the manager's eyes sinister? Wasn't Douglas? And what about this drooping, round-shouldered peacock? No, he wasn't sinister – merely ridiculous, like myself. Life was a cheerless business for the both of us. I began to miss him when he was not around.

Sometimes, he would buck up. When his shoulders straightened I knew the motorbikes were coming, though it was always before I could detect their drone. For the first couple of days I left as soon as his mates poured in, tall lads ducking out of their helmets, tugging at the fasteners on their black, studded gear, rowdy, sniffing and wet – always wet from the rain. But then I took to staying and I watched them play darts, larking, making to kick and punch and karate-chop, eating crisps noisily as kids, high-spirited, not bothering about me. With Ceri Griff there in their midst, uneasily silent – gauche cock-of-the-walk among the half-dyed crew-cuts and streaky spiky mops, and the sloppy manners and the rude wit. All their fooling annoyed him as it annoyed me. He wanted to get on with the game, and I wanted him to win.

I might have understood nothing of the language they spoke, but the figures they chalked up on the blackboard were my figures as much as theirs and gradually I came to know the rules. In general they threw the little feathered missiles either with an aggressiveness that made me wince, or with an affected boredom that I mistrusted. But one of them seemed to play, too, with malice. He would tot up Ceri's score wrongly or bump up the score of his nearest rivals. I felt like strangling Ceri for not even noticing.

I got so maddened on one occasion, when I caught the cheat winking, that I went up to the board, grabbed the chalk out of his hand, obliterated his score with a sidelong swipe of my fist and inserted the correct figures in neat, heavy numerals (I was after all far more experienced at writing on a blackboard than he was). Everything stopped, like a still from a film. Even the girl behind the bar stared. But nobody altered my score.

After that, when I noticed a mistake on the board, I pointed it out. Most of them would ignore me, but there was always some-one who would check the figures and then change them. After a while they simply went up and changed them, without bothering to check what I said.

On days when the gang didn't turn up, Douglas would summon Ceri to play, and then it was quite another matter. I would not even watch. I couldn't bear the way Douglas produced the pretty little weapons and snapped his fingers to alert Ceri; nor the way Ceri immediately rose, like some hypnotised hen. For if Douglas's scorn of me was expressed by an exaggerated courteousness now, his contempt for Ceri was undisguised. When the boy began winning, as he invariably did, Douglas would egg him on in tones you would use to goad a horse or a dog into attempting the impossible, for a joke. I was glad I could not understand what he was saying. I loathed the fellow, and I'm sure I showed it. But Ceri gave no sign of being tempted to stab his tormentor, nor of being provoked into wild feats. He played coolly on, under control, silent. I didn't know whether to admire him for his iron will, or get exasperated with him for being so thick he couldn't see what Douglas was at. The exasperation tended to dominate. For when Ceri was on the point of winning, Douglas would throw in his

40

feathers and turn away scoffing – scoffing at the game and scoffing at Ceri's seriousness about it. And Ceri would just stand there, looking pathetically half-witted under his plumage, his white neck poking forward like a half-plucked fowl's over the cave of his chest: asking, almost, for Douglas to humiliate him. Dear, dear.

But really, it was only the way society led you on into doing things and then turned on you and scoffed, and had no time for what you were doing. And slinking off to sulk in a corner when it happened wasn't that much nobler than standing there looking gormless. Hardly nobler at all. Just as ignoble, in fact.

When I came to the hotel, I thought I would be able to hold out for the month. But what with the whisky that seemed necessary, and one thing and another (and Douglas), I could see I was not going to manage. I would have to crawl back and accept the paltry offerings from the place where I had taken such a stand against the termination of earnings-related benefit. So I nerved myself to Ceri's passive acceptance of humiliation and went back.

It took me all day, a Wednesday. The buses were so awkward I had to miss breakfast, and it was late in the evening when I returned. The next morning the manager remarked cheerfully: 'We missed you yesterday.'

'Thought I'd done a bunk did you?'

'Ceri Griffiths was asking where you were, that's all.'

I wished I were young enough to feel aggressive about my lack of money, or old enough to slump into unawareness of it. As it was, I worried, uselessly and hopelessly, straying again and again down the crooked corridors as though I expected them to lead somewhere, and glancing out of every window as though I expected it to afford a different view. But wherever I went, I ended up back where I started, and wherever I looked, there were the bins and the puddles and the fire-escapes surmounting them like a gigantic, interminable game of snakes and ladders.

Continued unemployment, I would think, was the curse. With the assets of half a working life wearing out as the colour was wearing out of my hair, I was going to end up with everything gone, huddling in some home or hostel on a meagre pension (except that at this rate pensions would disappear before I laid my hands on one). If, by this time, I had reached the attic, I tended to discard all that as a fanciful, self-indulgent worry that had nothing on the operation, the likelihood of malignancy, the likelihood of recurrence – fears that had lain dormant under the blows of unemployment on the lower floors.

Worries, it seemed, were as contrary as the common cold. Put up any resistance and they fought back and wore you down. But submit, and indulge them for a while, and they were soon done with. Though the sooner then did they recur, of course. . .

Clearly, there was going to be no calm of a maturing sense of perspective.

What there was, however, was a distant hubbub. A Western on television? I went down to find it and I heard it above me: when I got the level right I wandered to and fro, hearing it first on my left then on my right. By the time I discovered Ceri playing one of the space-invader machines in the desolate dance-hall I was in a foul mood and ready to challenge the manager over his notions of 'soundproofing'. At the sight of Ceri I felt inclined to leave, but then I remembered he had asked for me when I was missing, and I went over to watch.

He stood in a bored, unexpectant way, apparently waiting for his space-ship to dock or refuel or get renewed in part-exchange or whatever. It looked a very elaborate game. Suddenly the machine burst into vehement stuttering and whining, and a long series of explosions. Ceri, it appeared, was deadly accurate. But his face had not changed. Far from expecting nothing to go his way, it seemed, he was assuming everything would.

For ages he stood there, massacring the enemy and dodging all the menace of the sky that a silicon chip could master-mind; and then he won a bonus game.

'Oh, well done!'

He ignored me and played monotonously on. I could imagine him as an ace pilot, bombing away with God-like unpertur-bability at those of us left clutching at the ground: it was reassuring to think that however much his skill was needed, no-one would ever bother to seek him out for it. Least of all here, buried in this sealed-off cavern, however unsoundproof.

'Wanna game?'

I was so taken aback that he spoke English, and so alarmed at the football game he had vaguely indicated that I got confused while refusing.

'You go that side.'

'Oh, yes, of course.'

He stood patiently waiting; and released the handles he was holding when I unwittingly grabbed the opposite ends of the same ones. In silence he moved over to the others.

'Am I white?' He said nothing. 'I'm white,' I insisted firmly.

He shot a goal.

'Hang on a moment. Which goal is it I'm aiming for?'

He pointed then.

'Ah,' I said, pretending all had been revealed.

It seemed that if you twiddled the handles constantly and indiscriminately, and if at the same time you jerked them madly in and out, your men on the field achieved, simply by some physical law of time and space, a degree of interaction with the ball that was not entirely humiliating.

In so doing, however, I seemingly agitated the contraption so violently it landed on his foot.

The shaving off of his eyebrows had left Ceri looking permanently startled. It was an expression accentuated now by his mouth falling open.

'I'm terribly sorry.'

Rudely, though he had already extricated his foot, he gave the field a savage shove in my direction. 'What are you doing here anyway?' he challenged.

'Same as you. Playing silly billies on this.'

'You know what I mean.'

'Well, I'm staying here. What are you doing?'

'Me? I stick around. Out of work, me.'

'Me too.'

'No.' It wasn't denial or astonishment, just a doubtful unwillingness to accept me in any category that included himself.

'Redundant,' I persisted.

'Oh well, I'm not redundant,' he protested, triumphantly distinguishing us. 'Never had work, see.'

'No loss. It doesn't do you a bit of good,' I heard myself comment bitterly.

It seemed to appease him.

'Sleep a lot do you?' he asked, sounding genuinely curious about how I got through my days.

'Sleep hardly at all. The place is haunted.'

'Yeh.' He grinned. 'I kept thinking that too. It turned out to be you.'

We hovered awkwardly. Ceri seemed to have got bored and I was anxious, because it was a while since I had last rinsed my mouth and I thought my breath had probably begun to smell. So we drifted away, from under elaborate lamps festooning the place like some deep-sea diving equipment, and from among the lost property and the stale beer surrounding us like urine samples.

'If we got told to do something with these glasses, I'd smash 'em up, but I bet you'd go and wash 'em up, wouldn't you?'

I said: 'Whereas, as things stand, we neither of us do anything about them.'

But he would not leave it at that. The same night, in the Hungry Cheese, he went over to the wall and unhooked from it the red and black picture, and carried it over to me ritualistically, as though this were to be the test of whether or not our paths really crossed.

'Can you see what this is?'

'Well, it's an abstract, isn't it?' The crude shapes seemed more infantile than ever. 'I don't like it, if that's what you mean.'

'But what's it a picture of?' He sounded so earnest I felt disconcerted.

'Amoebae under a microscope, perhaps? I don't know. What?'

He clicked his tongue, impatient with me, annoyed, and went to hang it up on its nail. Back on his perch with his beer, a look of dismal satisfaction crept across his face.

I was the more surprised when he took it down from the wall again later that evening and pressed it upon his mates. He refused to take the darts from them, insisted and pleaded, with more animation in his small, neat features than I had ever seen. For a

44

moment the others were vaguely embarrassed by it; then, uninterested, they played on without him.

All that my blindness had aroused in him was scorn, but the blindness of his mates caused him pathetic disappointment.

I didn't watch their games of darts that evening: I stared and stared at the wall. Into the red and black shapes there I traced every conceivable kind of landscape and of portrait and of still life, but the picture never became anything more than what it seemed – a lot of inartistic, meaningless, floating patches. In the end I gave up: I couldn't concentrate for the whisky: I would come back, as soon as the Hungry Cheese opened in the morning, and peruse the frustrating thing through sober eyes.

Just before closing-time, an unkempt man joined the gang. He was older than them and not of their breed; his blond hair and blue tie-dyed T-shirt stood out oddly from their garish hair and studs and black plastic (or was it leather got up to look like plastic?). Yet they clustered around him and listened to him as though he had some kind of authority, and when Ceri took the picture from the wall and offered it to him, he got his reward. For the unkempt man did no more than glance at it before he looked up and spoke, and Ceri withdrew the design and hung it for a third time on its nail, this time with an expression of quiet gratification on his face.

Obscurely, I felt that yet again I had missed my chance.

CHAPTER FOUR

I began to spend rather a lot of time in the Hungry Cheese, and as little as possible in my room. I felt cooped up there, in my room, bricked up almost, like that small furry thing I had touched, crouching unsuspected in the heart of the brickwork, buried alive. By day I would listen to the casual, free life lived the other side of the walls and by night to the urgent, muffled goings-on on the scaffolding behind the curtains, as though stage-hands changed sets between the acts of my dreams. Or else my skin would creep with the sensation of being watched, and I would be unable to rid myself of the uncomfortable feeling that the room had eyes, like a prisoner's cell. The walls of the Hungry Cheese, on the other hand, were indubitably solid.

There were not even any windows in them, for flies to gather at and crawl up, as they crawled in my room, rubbing their hind legs together, as if to shake off their contact with the bundle of broken bodies on the sill below. They were insects ripe for the picking – alive, just, but without any means of evading the crude tactics of such little boys as make a habit of harvesting their wings and legs. Gangs of little boys getting bigger and older. (Little girls did it as well, obviously, but not openly and not in groups, aware already that their cruelty was not met with the same resigned tolerance as their brothers'. In secret and alone, and with a more exquisite shame, they did the things that made them witches still – or bitches, or whatever expletive was currently fashionable.)

The lads in the Hungry Cheese had doubtless been just such a gang, of course, but they were an easy crowd to be among. They made no demands on me, but they would nevertheless acknowledge, now and again, that I was around.

I even came to like the way that, without understanding a word, I was growing familiar with them, as one can become familiar

46

with animals, whose minds are still closed books.

I began to believe they were accepting my presence, too. Not for comfort, as theirs comforted me, but as children accept their mother's presence when they come into the kitchen looking for someone else and with their minds on higher things – taking her for granted, and not needing her any more, but irritated if she isn't where she usually is, and so where she somehow ought to be.

Not that they didn't exclude me rudely enough, huddling so tightly in a corner that even the walls seemed to be giving way under their pressure. They would rise as out of a mould, leaving the imprint of their shoulders and backs in the plaster: one groove had become so niche-like that much later, on the night of the storm, Aled and I set a candle in it.

But for the time being, the manager would briskly flick the light-switch. It was hardly subtle lighting, coming from a single naked bulb strung up to the central beam; but it was so old, that bulb, and its dusty glass was so grey, it didn't give a harsh glare, just a gloomy yellowy light, that had to battle through the pall of cigarette smoke perpetually drifting to the ceiling or hanging in strands around the room.

I sat at the bar sometimes, if the manager was serving.

'He's got a lost look about him, Ceri Griff, hasn't he?'

'Aye – moons around doesn't he? Since the day he got disqualified.'

'Disqualified?'

'Aye. Copped for speeding and then found to be driving an unroadworthy machine not taxed or insured. The usual story.' He was pulling pints for Ceri's pals, who had just appeared, leaning back, looking down his nose, and setting the full glasses up on the counter as grimly as if he had been their father. His voice had assumed a fatalistic note.

When he was free again I asked: 'Is it only since he's had no bike then, that he's seemed the odd one out?'

'Ceri Griff? Oh, Ceri Griff's alright.' A contrary man, the manager.

'Lonely though.'

'Well, who isn't, these days?'

'It's different when you're young though.'

'Ceri Griff's alright,' he repeated, adding under his breath: 'It's not him's the bother.' I noticed with surprise the brawny forearms and the grubbiness of the rolled-up sleeves. I had got used to thinking of him as thin and well-dressed.

'He's very good at those space-invader machines, you know.'

'Oh those.'

'It seems such a waste.'

'He wouldn't be much good at dealing with any less fanciful kind of invasion, let me tell you. There's none of them would.'

'How d'you mean?'

'What they need, youngsters like that, is a bit of real trouble. That'd cure them. All this fancy messing-about and play-acting! Cloud-cuckoo-land they live in.'

'How d'you mean?'

He leaned over the bar. 'What that lot needed was to be sent to the Falklands. Conscripted and sent. They'd none of them go of their own accord to a real war.'

'The Falklands? Real war?'

'They don't know what war is, that lot. And they think they do – that's their trouble.'

'That seems rather a strong condemnation of space-invader machines. Especially coming from someone who profits from them.'

He looked at me for a second as though he pitied me, then his expression became wary, as though he suspected me more of deviousness than imbecility.

'They think they know, that's what's wrong with them. But they don't – they have no idea.'

He ended so ferociously, I dropped the subject. Perhaps, after all, he was remembering the Second World War. He was hardly old enough to have fought in it, but he might easily have lost his family in it. Come as an evacuee to this remote part of Wales, like so many others, and stayed, with no-one to go back to when peace was made. A little boy with a gasmask, awkwardly getting down from the train, the luggage-label askew on his jersey, bearing an address that had been blown to smithereens.

He was tearing packets of peanuts off a card as though he were skinning a rabbit.

'Is he local, Ceri Griff?'

'Oh he's local alright.' It was affirmed with the satisfaction of a man who had got him where he could keep an eye on him. Or possibly the resignation of a man who saw no chance of ever shaking him off. It was hard to tell which. Not that they weren't quite compatible, of course, for a rat is more likely to get its teeth into you when you have it cornered.

'Why didn't his mates get copped too?'

'Oh they've got machines now, haven't they?' he suggested. 'They're not riding around on broken bits of rusty metal, them.' He wiped the counter down as though it were a butcher's slab. 'Never had a chance, Ceri Griff, never from a child.'

'Why was that, then?'

'Oh, his mother you know.' His nose wrinkled in disgust, either at the thought of the mother or at a whiff from his dishrag. 'Not that she had much choice either, I suppose.' He wrung out the cloth, raising it high above the sink, as if to savour the grey matter trickling from it. 'There's just her and him – always been just her and him. It goes hard on the kid, that's certain.'

I absorbed this in silence, imagining his mother, my sort of age.

'Not that I like the boy, mind you,' he reassured me, staring hard with those black and white eyes that were all pupil and no iris, as I stood up (the dishrag had reminded me that I ought to swill out my mouth). 'No I couldn't say that now,' I heard him murmur to himself behind me. 'I couldn't indeed.'

His reaction to Ceri might swing as incomprehensively as an opinion poll, but mine, as I stooped over the basin, was patronisingly steadfast. It wasn't out of our fifth form we should have recruited for our sixth: it was out of the ballrooms of large, run-down hotels, out of pubs and discos and fairgrounds – hauling out those gifted freaks who had no chance, by their hairless scruffs. A deep ache broke through the numbness of the left side of my face and I felt old, old. How I could dream like that, persisting in the brave new world of the Sixties when I was in such a state, heaven only knew. The Sixties, for God's sake! As though anything that had blossomed in that brief spring could have survived this kind of a summer! Rain in August rotted seed as surely as autumn followed. And no matter how mellow that autumn, nothing could reverse its barrenness then.

'What'll happen to him?' I asked, back at the bar, drawing my finger through the counter's smears.

'Oh he'll get caught, I imagine. Jail then.' He spoke with a weary indifference, but I was taken aback.

'He's still riding that bike then?'

The hotelier looked at me as though he couldn't make me out. 'It's a bit more sinister than that,' he commented drily.

'Sinister?' I forgot, for a moment, why it struck a chord. 'You shouldn't immediately assume. . .', assume? Assume or conclude? Conclude? Assume? I must be going senile, to forget what had been reverberating for three weeks from cell to cell of my brain as from stone to stone around some whispering gallery. The one intelligible sentence I had had to go on – for by the time they asked if there was anything I wanted to ask, I was even more senile than now.

Not like the man in some other room I had passed while looking for the way out, the man who was telling them angrily to cut all the jargon and tell him straight, with no more messing about: did he, or did he not, have cancer? I had stood listening so intently I could hear the subdued medical tones smoothly alleging they did not think in such terms. At an abrupt thump I had jumped. 'Yes or no!' insisted the patient, and you would have sworn he held them at gunpoint. 'Well then, yes.' God help him, I thought, God help him – at least he tried to resist! But he wasn't done. After a silence, he lost control. How dare they just sit there, and tell him, just like that? How did they know he was psychologically fit to know? Had they agonised over whether he should be told or not, taken everything into consideration? Not on your life. They had just sat there and casually come out with it. For all they knew, he might go straight off and commit suicide. He had a good mind to show them. And they needn't think they could hush it up – he would write to all the papers first. He knew what coroners were!

Then, by miraculous transference, you are out on the street, a newly-born abandoned baby. Filled with a huge anticipation and a suction-pad that is creating, of your stomach, a vacuum.

I nodded to the manager, who had indicated my empty glass. 'Miss Thomas,' he confirmed with distant courteousness as he set before me the raw, ripe, mesmerising gold. I grinned at him while he scooped together the debased coins. 'It's a fine name,' he said, so facetiously I was able to ask: 'What's yours?'

'Same as yours.' He had his back to me, dropping the money into the till, and I was overcome by a moment's anxiety lest he had thought I had been offering to buy him a drink. But he did not pour himself one and I took it he had been referring, after all, to his name. But I didn't know whether he meant he was Thomas something, or something Thomas, so I still couldn't call him anything.

Ceri and his mates were ensconced on the corner bench, under the sad red and black scraps on the wall. They were engrossed in something they held below the rim of their beer-barrel table; so engrossed, I could stare, that afternoon, with impunity. But they were sniggering over it, in that rather excited, shame-faced way that a batch of silly teenagers will snigger, and I was glad I didn't have to deal with that sort of thing any more. One of the few perks of redundancy.

Whenever my namesake went anywhere near them, they made a great to-do of bundling whatever it was up someone's jacket, creating such a suggestive bulge it set them all off again. It seemed to be only some magazine or other and the manager seemed quite resigned to their silliness, but they began to get on my nerves after a while – so much so, I almost wished I was still in a position to go over and confiscate the blessed thing.

I got nowhere by glowering, for when he was with the others Ceri affected not to notice me. If he did accidentally catch my eye, his embarrassment was always plain, but he was taking precautions to avoid such an accident now. I could have sat there for hours and had no effect at all. His fair-haired, denimed, clair-voyant friend, however, had only to appear in the doorway for Ceri's face to change completely. He chucked the magazine under the bench and flung a jacket down on it while the others sat as if stupefied. This was serious concealment now.

The older, bitter-looking man was so wiry even his narrow jeans hung baggily on him. Lithely as a snake, he insinuated himself between their legs and retrieved the magazine. He laid it down very deliberately on the barrel-top, but he did not so much as glance at it. He surveyed them a moment, spoke quickly and tensely, and left. He must have learnt young, I thought, to stare fiercely out of those deep-set eyes, to forestall any tendency in humankind to laugh at the overhanging eyebrows, that looked like a handlebar moustache severed down the middle, inverted, and glued to his forehead. The gang collected their jackets and followed like zombies, not daring to lift the magazine, not even behind his back.

It was nearly three o'clock and I was all that was left and the manager had disappeared.

I rather surprised myself by walking across the room.

But it was none of the *Playboys* or the *Penthouses* I had long ago raked in by the dozen, that lay on the barrel – it was an old copy of *Woman's Own*. Open at an article on contraception that their mothers might have read with misgivings and their sisters with avid anxiety.

It was only then it struck me that they never brought girls into the Hungry Cheese.

Indeed, I was not aware of any other women in the hotel at all, apart from staff and dining-guests. For all the evidence of life outside the walls of my room, it was always male life. The heavy, confident tread in the carpeted corridors, the hearty voices there, the throat-clearing and coughing and gargling at other basins – all of it was male; so was the pattering of feet and the broken whispering on the fire-escape in the dark. No matter how I strained to hear, they were not once followed by the lighter, quicker, more tentative sounds of women. Was I the only woman staying in the entire place? Or were there others lying doggo like me, caged like mice and never heard? At times I would think so, as when the schoolboy dispensing clean linen handed me a towel with a smear of lipstick in one corner. But I had not the heart to

52

complain; he had been agitated as a squirrel at the door, and if he'd somehow boobed with the whole batch, he must have spent hours folding everything to conceal the crumples and stains. . .

Then, too, I would catch, in the corridors, faint whiffs of perfume – whiffs that couldn't comfortably be put down to men's colognes or scented furniture polishes. Any time I retraced my steps though, they had gone. And it began to seem uncanny that it was always on corners that I caught them, these whiffs, as though the women had hung back there and hesitated before facing whatever was round the bend. As though it had been myself each time that had passed that way. And yet all I left behind me these days, I hoped, was the odour of mouthwashes.

Usually, all that was round the corner, if anything was, was Ceri.

'Do you play pool?' he asked aggressively one day when it was too late for him to slip into a room or down another passage, or pretend he hadn't seen me. He confessed, rather irritably, to half remembering noticing a pool table somewhere and feeling half inclined to give it a go. So instead of each of us wandering witlessly round the bewildering alleys on our own, we patrolled them together, and whether out of irritation at having got himself saddled with me or what, Ceri began searching in earnest and we did finally turn up the table, upended in a room stacked with junk.

'Come on – let's heave it into the middle – have you got any cash on you?'

'What are all these funny holes doing everywhere?'

'Holes? What holes?' He was peering crossly at the table. 'You need holes for the balls to go down.'

'No – in the wall, like there. They're all over the place.'

'Oh those. That's where they ripped the old gas fires from. If you haven't got any cash we can't play.'

When I saw the coloured balls obediently pop out the hole and line up in a demure crocodile, I laughed. Ceri scowled and said: 'Where are the cues?'

We hunted round a bit and then Ceri kicked relentlessly at the door of a cupboard that kept falling open. 'We'll just have to drop the idea, then, won't we?'

But I was aggrieved at the loss of my twenty pence and wouldn't commit myself.

'What d'you want that for?' I was propping myself up on a walking stick I had found.

'Well, wouldn't it do?'

'What, that?' He went out, banging the door in disgust.

By the time I'd got the balls (less obedient now) organised into an approximate triangle, he was behind me again. I smashed the triangle with a good deal of satisfaction.

'You playing?'

'Oh, alright.'

'You needn't – I'm quite happy pottering around on my own.'

He scattered the balls a bit more and examined, critically, the stick's rubber tip.

To take his mind off it, I asked: 'Who's the man under the eyebrows that's been in the Hungry Cheese the past couple of days?'

'Aled you mean?' He was immediately on the defensive.

'I don't know. Do I?' I leaned over the table in what I felt to be a professional stance. It was ineffectual.

'Aled,' he confirmed, more submissively.

He was the only person I was ever to hear call him 'Aled'. To everyone else he was always 'Aled Owen' just as Ceri was always 'Ceri Griff' – even to Aled.

'You – and the others – you kind of hero-worship him, don't you?'

'No.' He potted one of the patterned balls, which meant, he insisted, that the plain balls were mine. 'Spotted – those are spotted.' I said nothing, it being quite plain they were not spotted.

It wasn't just the coiffure and the eyebrowlessness that made him look like a chicken; it was his sharp nose and receding chin and the way his scraggy neck craned, thrusting his head forward and cocking it a little to one side, quizzically.

'He's been inside, see,' he burst out, long after I had forgotten Aled.

'I see.' I must have sounded prim, for his pasty face turned sulky, and to stop him marching off again I assured him flatteringly: 'You all look as if you've been inside for years. You all need feeding up good and proper.'

His wry grin surprised me – it seemed so tired. It was the kind of grin his mother must have been very familiar with.

'Funny place for you to be then – with a load of ex-convicts,' he commented, more curious than sarcastic.

'Hey, stop messing.' It was my shot, but he was grinding the tip of the walking stick into some school chalk he had got hold of, and it was crumbling onto the table.

'Oh, sorry.' He blew it away and then looked at the watch on my wrist – but it was a nothing kind of time, as usual.

'Come on.'

'Right.' He handed over the stick. 'Funny you coming here.'

'So you keep saying. Oh, goal, good. Why is it funny?' I felt better, with one pocketed.

'Dunno. Coming on your own, like.'

'I can come on my own.'

'A Welsh place, this.'

'I am Welsh.'

'No.'

I couldn't help thinking that the mark Ceri was making, rubbing the table with the finger he had spat on, probably did the baize as little good as my stab at it with the walking stick. As it was the stab he was trying to erase, I kept quiet, but I was amused by his sudden concern for the table. 'I don't think you are supposed to do that,' he said. 'You shouldn't go berserk just because you're losing.'

'You can be Welsh without speaking it.'

'No.'

'There's no "no" about it. You just can, and I am. And that's that.'

'How many English people do you know who can't speak English?' He potted a spotty, and I got two goes. 'Be a bit funny, somebody who could only speak French telling you he was English wouldn't it?'

He was so worked up he didn't notice me pot the black.

Provocation seemed, in the circumstances, healthier than confession. 'Wales is bilingual,' I asserted authoritatively.

'How long have you been on the dole anyway?' This, it appeared, didn't require an answer. 'Hey – where's the black?' This, it became clear, did.

'Black?'

'The black ball?'

'What black ball?'

'The black ball.'

'We never had any black ball.'

'We must of.'

'No we never.'

'Oh well, that does it. You can't play without the black.'

'Don't be so soft – we're playing without the cues, aren't we?'

'Yeh, but. . . well I hope no-one catches us, that's all.'

'A very noble sentiment coming from an admirer of criminals, but may I remind you we've paid.'

'Yeh, but. . .'

'Four bob in old money, that.'

'Was it?' Ceri considered. 'You must've known Elvis the Pelvis and all that.'

'The bloke who advised a wooden chair in the absence of a partner.' Ceri found this so funny I hastily clarified the context. 'God knows how he jived – personally, I found a door gave you a lot more scope.' When he found this funnier still, I gave up. 'Come on.'

'Okay. Okay. I've only got the pink left to pot you know.'

'Well, hurry up and then you can help me with mine.'

'Don't be daft, mun.' The last stripey was lurking behind a spotty, and he missed. 'I suppose the Beatles were hot stuff in your day?'

'I suppose they were.'

'I heard people on about them when I was little and I thought they were talking about beetles. Then we had the death-watch beetle, and I said "yes" when anyone asked if I'd heard the Beatles.' He added: 'There was only me mam and me so we had them fucking beetles for years.'

56

'Gracious – I wonder what you must have made of the Rolling Stones?'

'They're great,' he enthused, and won.

I carried on smacking away at my spotties, without zeal, but there was another hour until opening time.

'You ever hear the death-watch beetle?' he asked.

'No.'

'You wanna come and see where I live. One hell of a hole. It's no wonder only the bloody English want it.' He started poking feebly among the junk enclosing us. There was no way of persuading him, in his hour of glory, to assist me.

'How d'you mean?'

'Me mam's trying to sell it, see,' he told me wearily, then tugged viciously at the leg of something buried. There was a rip, and a clutter of readjustment.

'Hey, go easy with that. Don't bust everything.'

'Everything's bust already.' Suddenly he perked up with a brightness as artificial as his hair. 'What you doing living in a hotel anyway? Wouldn't yer fancy a wee, olde worlde little Welsh stone cottage, tucked among them hills? Very fashionable – well, the other side the border anyway.'

'With the rattle of the death-watch beetle.'

'You're prejudiced – you never heard one. They're good company.' His buoyance collapsed. 'No, the beetles are gone, but you're no good anyway, are you? You've got no money, have you?'

'No.'

'D'you know anyone who would have?' There was a be-seeching edge to his voice, and he stopped fiddling to listen to my reply, though he didn't look round.

'No, I'm afraid I don't,' I said softly. 'Why does she want to sell?'

'Wants to move into town. There's this flat going. She's half-crippled, like. Arthritis. Can't walk from the bus-stop.'

'Oh dear.'

'Used to take her on the back of the bike – bike fell to bits. There's this Wolverhampton burk wants the house.' He stood

57

there pouting, a child tricked into betraying a confidence.

'That sounds like the solution, then.'

'No, I won't.'

'Why not?'

'I can't.'

'Why?'

'Well, do you think it's right, letting the English buy up our heritage for their holiday homes?'

'Sounds as though you read that somewhere.'

'It's what me mates think too. And you know what happens when places get sold for holiday homes.' Fear had crept into his voice.

I stared. 'You don't think your mates would really do anything do you?'

He hung his head, as if I had reproved him. 'No. Aled's promised.' But he sounded unhappy and uncertain.

'Aled?'

'Yeh – he told me I'm not to feel under pressure.' I snorted. 'No, he's going to keep them off. Honest. It's my free decision.' He paused, as if waiting for me to snort again, but I was silent. 'He's going to keep them off,' he repeated.

'And you trust him?'

'Yes.'

'But would he be able to?' Douglas bent on trouble might be a handful even for Aled.

'I dunno quite. . .' He looked pathetic and helpless – weak, I suppose. 'He might – until the sale's gone through anyway.'

'Ceri, why on earth don't you grow your eyebrows – just your eyebrows?' I pleaded.

'I'm not doing everything my mother wants!'

'Then you shouldn't expect her to do everything you want.'

'What?'

'Does she need your permission to sell the cottage?'

'No, but I've said I won't go into the flat with her if she sells to the English. I can hang around here – often sleep here now. . . as you know,' he remembered suddenly, grinning – but it was a defeated grin that soon faded, and there were tears in his eyes as he looked down.

'No, what I meant was – couldn't you convince your mates it was against your wishes, this sale? Nothing to do with you.'

'You think that'd wash?' He was appalled at my naiveté. 'You know nothing.' He turned his back and started rummaging – a rabbit burrowing.

'Christ, you're bleedin' dangerous with that thing,' he shouted when a ball hit him in the back (I had taken to whacking them, as the more depleted they became the less impact I was managing to make on them).

'Beware of an armed woman.' I waved the stick crossly at him, like an old lady chasing a punk out of her cabbage-bed, and he laughed. 'Another game?'

But he was having no more pool. 'I'm tired,' he kept complaining.

'You should get some sleep.'

'I get lots of sleep.'

'Not at night you don't.'

He looked at me sharply, but seemed reassured, by what he saw, that I was only guessing.

After a pause, as if to startle me in return, he said: 'Well, if you're looking for sleep tonight, you've had it.'

'If I'm looking for sleep any night, I've had it.'

'No,' he said, considering, determined to be fair.

'What's on tonight then?'

'We've a load coming in – we hope.'

'Load?'

'Fertilizer.' He looked up smugly as he sauntered towards the door. 'Good farming country all round here you know – very good.' He smacked his thin lips theatrically, making a dimple come incongruously to his white cheek.

'Can't be that good if it needs so much fertilizer,' I said and he laughed.

'Me mate, Douglas, thinks you're a spy.'

'What do you think?'

'I think you know more than you let on.' He surveyed me through narrow eyes, sizing me up mockingly. 'I think you might even know Welsh, you're that secretive.' His mood changed abruptly again. 'But I don't think you're spying.'

After potting, or putting, or pooling, or whatever, like that, I could hardly be expected to be up to it.

CHAPTER FIVE

When I went to the Hungry Cheese that evening, someone was already there. I was taken aback – it was barely half-past five and I had got used to being the first customer. The occupant was, moreover, installed where I always sat. An old man with a small head and large hands, who looked round and greeted me in Welsh. There was no-one behind the bar and he didn't have a drink. But the fire had been lit.

I sat on the other settle, opposite him, watching the logs twinkle and splinter in the young flames. There was no heat from them yet, but the old man moved his legs away at the slightest hiss or crackle.

When he spoke again, I ignored him.

'*Wyt ti'n siarad Cymraeg?*' he persisted.

I shook my head.

He ignored me then, tipping back his peaked tweed cap and scratching slowly among the few white hairs across the top of his forehead. The line between his wizened, weather-beaten face and smooth pink scalp made his baldness look like a bad case of stage make-up. As if aware of this, he settled his cap comfortably back.

'Will we get served, do you think?' he asked the ceiling eventually, in ponderous doubt.

I was relieved when the manager appeared, but he treated us both coldly.

When he saw the molten gold in the glass I was brought, the old man perked up. 'Whisky?' His neck came out from his collar as if his head was on a swivel-stick, and the little button eyes pricked. 'That's the devil's own drink, that.'

I agreed.

He was wearing moleskin trousers that were of a complex shape quite unrelated to his anatomy: they creaked whenever his anatomy presumed to interfere with it. Perhaps it was they made his head look too small for his body.

'You want to watch that you know.' The head wobbled, awkward and precarious.

'Oh I do – I spend hour upon hour watching it.'

'What's that?' The head stuck at a tilt, its little piggy eyes squinting into the distance to hear better.

'I said, I spend a long time. . .'

'No – that – that. . .' It was the red and black shapes on the wall behind me that were agitating him.

'Modern art.'

'Eh? Eh? You're not from these parts are you?' He spoke as though I had brought the picture in with me.

'Can't you see what it is?' I asked him.

'What?'

'That picture. What is it a picture of? Can't you see?'

The proprietor, for some reason, was making a lot of noise behind the bar. I couldn't see how there could be glasses to swill at opening time, or why he had to dry them until they squeaked to set your teeth on edge.

'Think it must be the ole bull when he's charging at one of them red things,' the old man pronounced at last.

Probably everyone interpreted it according to his own life-style – in which case it was no wonder it remained unidentifiable to me.

He began collecting mucus hoarsely in his throat. I expected him to lean forward and gob into the logs, but he swallowed it instead. He was only being polite, I suppose, but it kept sticking in his throat and he would have to retrieve it and try swallowing it again.

I found myself clearing my own throat to try and drown the noise of his.

I was glad when I heard the squealing of bike brakes.

Three of the youngsters came in and made straight for the dartboard. When one of them noticed the old man, he nudged and whispered to one of the others, who stopped and looked round and shrugged, then carried on.

The old man's neck, visible again, was blotchy and a rather

62

dark red. It shrank back only when one lad came up and offered him the feathered ends of the darts.

'Not from these parts, are you?' he sneered again. My presence must have been as irksome to him as his was to me. 'Got a dog here have you?' he accused.

'Dogs are not allowed in this hotel,' the manager called over severely.

'Huh, there's dogs enough in this hotel.' It was a low growl, but savage.

'What can you mean?' I asked, loudly and coldly.

The old man sagged, as though accepting the rebuke, but his pride must have rebelled. 'Whole place has gone to the dogs if you ask me,' he muttered and he spat out the next mouthful of mucus before I could look away. It spread glistening on the ash, then began writhing and bubbling in the heat. 'Dogs got at my sheep this year,' he lamented, kicking the logs as a cat will scratch the earth it has used, 'whole flock of them. Eighteen lambs I lost, you know; took eighteen lambs off me. And five sheep. Up from those blasted caravans at Derwen-las, I shouldn't wonder. Eighteen lambs. Still. . .' He looked up more chirpily, though his palms still rubbed each other so hard I could see the flakes of skin falling like powder on his clothes. 'I suppose if you've got one it'll be a poodle or a pekinese or suchlike. Or a corgi,' he added, his face darkening again, 'and they're a menace too, for all their royal connections.' His bitter laugh released more phlegm from his lungs. 'Do you think I'd be in here now,' he asked me fiercely, making it sound like prison, 'if it hadn't been for that damn dog of yours? Do you?' He leaned towards me urgently and I shook my head. 'No sir,' he confirmed, saluting in mock dignity from the peak of his cap. 'But I'm too old for it now. Can't stay up with a gun all night, these days. Not like these young beggars now.' He folded his arms to survey them with a patronising envy. 'Never done a day's work in their lives, that lot, you know,' he informed me confidentially, adding with satisfied contempt: 'Don't know what work is. Couldn't work, no matter what they was paid.'

'Ah, but it's we're paying you, isn't it?' Aled had come up behind him, to lay a hand on the old shoulder. He spoke with

63

quiet pleasantness, but the old man's manner became servile – unresistingly he got up to go where he was bid.

As he passed me, Aled caught my eye, and I saw him recognise me. It seemed he had shaved off a beard or a moustache, for despite the eyebrows his face seemed less hairy than when he was shouting at me, up the slope behind the Abbey, a man undaunted by Christ, ready, with the rock in his fist, to cast the first stone at the erring woman.

With Aled had come Douglas and Ceri; Ceri winked at me as he followed the others into the far corner of the room, behind me. The dart-playing trio gathered there too: only the manager, still furiously polishing his glasses, wiping his shelves (lifting the bottles even), and wringing out his rags, did not join the group.

Through the murmur of their voices came the old man's whining, on and on, grating, infuriating. Now and then it broke out into unashamed pleading, or naked fear, or rough anger, rising over the soft background hum that seemed to menace him like a hive of wasps. I sat tensely waiting for each outburst to end, and for each lull to crack.

They were bargaining with him, but it was difficult to make out what more was going on. I looked across when I got up for another drink: the old man was wheedling with a half-sly smile on his face, but he was dribbling and his flannel shirt protruded through his open jacket where force had been used.

When the manager, evidently sharing my misgivings, walked over to take their order, Douglas swore at him, so then he had to make do with crossing to and fro between me and the bar. As I was equally anxious to make the same journey on the same pretext, we collided more than once and I ended up drinking rather more than I intended.

The second time I got up, Douglas was obscuring the old man, bending so that their faces must have nearly touched. The old man was shrinking back, his hands working over the knees of his moleskins, kneading them like a cat.

The third time, the old man was leaning forward, openly slavering and shaking (it was hard to tell whether in greed or in fear), with the others around him in a huddle, baiting him. I wondered if, after the operation (when the nerve already damaged in my face would be permanently destroyed, and the muscles weakened), I would have as little control over my features when calm, as he had over his when anguished.

I suddenly felt I wanted nothing more to do with the whole pack of them, and I left before closing-time.

When I heard the knock at my door, the first person who came to mind was the manager, for I knew he had seen me fall as I stumbled up the steps out of the Hungry Cheese.

'Who is it?'

'Can I come in? Can I come in please?'

Giddy as I felt, I was puzzled for only a moment – the farmer, agitated, lost, desperate as his sheep for asylum from his pursuing predators.

'Quick.' Somehow I got him inside (despite the doorway's strange liability to subside) and locked the door. He looked alarmed. 'Are you alright?' I asked.

'Yes. . .' He licked his lips nervously, as though his mouth had gone dry with fear. 'I think so. I think I'm alright. How – how are you?' The silly man seemed scared of me, even.

'Well, you deserved all that, letting them play games with you like that. I knew it would turn nasty: you're too old to cope with that sort of thing from the likes of them. Running rings round you right from the start.'

He sat down on the bed. 'Don't be like that,' he coaxed, and then coyly: 'I got a good price you know.'

'Never mind the price you're getting, look at the price you're paying.'

He sat rubbing his hands, seeming to go off into a daydream. 'Yes, I did get a good price out of it. . .' Abruptly he came back to reality. 'Look, sit down.' He tapped the covers beside him with his tough black nails: 'Sit down.'

I couldn't make him out, but I did desperately need to sit down, and if he was none too clear in the head, then neither was I.

'Look – how far behind you are they?'

'Eh? What? Behind me?' He turned to look behind him. 'You're a rum one. Relax. Let's drink to it.'

65

Only then did it dawn on me he might be seeking celebration rather than refuge. Maybe I was so paranoid myself, I imagined everyone else needed help too.

'You've already drunk to it. Can we get this straight, please: are they or are they not looking for you?'

'Er. . .' I saw him turn over in his mind the reply that would be most to his advantage. 'I couldn't honestly say now, I'm sure. You wouldn't know what they was up to, that lot. They could well be looking for me.' He stroked his stubbly chin as if contemplating this idea.

I got up to unlock the door and he grabbed my arm, making me fall sideways onto the bed again. 'Now just a minute,' I protested (as much to the room, which was in motion, as to him). But his knobbly fingers dug into my waist and I couldn't think with the hot blasts of his beery breath on my face. Where the white stubble was you couldn't see his blood vessels, but above it the network of little capillaries seemed to be bursting through his skin, and his purplish nose looked damp and bloated. Down either side of it tears ran, out of weak eyes whose whites looked old and smoke-stained. They ran to join the shining slug-trails of dried-up spittle either side of his mouth. I slapped him, hard.

It was like salt on a leech. He seemed to shrivel up. Once again I went to open the door, but as I got up, the room set off too, in the opposite direction, and I found myself clutching the basin to hold it back. He was behind me before I knew, his heavy hands on my shoulders, propelling me back to the bed.

'Hey there, take it easy now. Take it easy. I don't know what you thought. We'll just have a little talk. There, there.' He seemed to be enjoying himself, carrying my two hands into his lap and patting them.

'Will you get out please.'

'Yes, yes, in a little while – just want to make sure you're alright.'

'I'll be alright as soon as you go.'

'Yes, yes.' But he kept patting my hands in a mechanical manner. He was grimacing like a gargoyle, and like a gargoyle's, his face was grotesque only till it struck you how comical, even pathetic, it was.

'You go away now. We both need a good night's sleep.'

'Yes, I'm going. Best to get warm first – it's very wet out there.' We listened to the rain, leaking from the guttering and through the fire-escapes, while I felt drunk and exhausted and ill, and had my hands patted.

'Nice to feel cosy, isn't it?' He snuggled closer. 'Nice to *cwtch* up,' he suggested in a grating whisper, 'isn't it?' The patting was getting perfunctory and irregular and absent-minded.

'No it is not. And now I'm afraid I must really ask you to go.' I stood up and faced him with my hands on my hips and my feet firmly apart for balance – blocking his way in fact, now I think of it.

For a moment he sat with his head bowed so that I could see the freckles under the powdery dandruff on his scalp. He was a man who could make you really believe that household dust is mostly human skin. His shoulders were hunched around his wax-looking ears, and his arms, rigid on either side of him, grasped the edge of the bed. He looked up, sorrowfully, and I sighed deeply in exasperation.

'Why are you like this?' He shook his head. 'Why is it? Poor woman.'

'I'm not explaining why. Are you going or are you not?' This was a mistake – it made him think he had a choice. He brightened up as he looked down the length of the bed. Then he swivelled round, swinging his feet up and lying back, folding his hands under his head.

'No.'

'Get those shoes off that bed.' His legs shot off as though by reflex action and he was left sitting in his earlier position, shaking his head in a befuddled way. I kept up the tone: 'Look at them.' He was already doing that. 'They've been through mud and manure and all sorts.' He opened his mouth to protest. 'And look at you. Just look at you.' He did his best, in a chagrined sort of way, but it was impossible to shame him: his imp-like manner returned and he cocked his head slyly.

'But you're the one I want to look at, lady.'

'This is infantile behaviour – a grown man like you.'

67

'Oh yes, I'm grown, lady.' There was an edge of aggression to his joking tone that made me drop the scorn.

'Unless you leave this instant, I am going to get the manager.' I sounded dangerous, but I didn't relish the thought of enlisting Thomas. Moreover, the Hungry Cheese would be closed, and I had no idea where he lived. The hotel would be locked up too. 'And you'll have to go out by the fire-escape.'

I strode over and unlocked the door, then strode to the window and opened that. The air that stirred the curtains was reasonably cool for a change.

'Are you throwing me out?'

'That's right.' I bustled back round the bed. 'You've got the idea. Now, out you go. Shoo.' I took hold of his arm peremptorily.

He yanked it from me, so ferociously that his elbow hit him in the ribs, winding him. 'Bitch. You bitch.' He began coughing, an ugly, moist, half-faked cough that sounded painful.

'Have you. . . got anything?' He was trying to catch the streams of saliva over the backs of his hands, but they still dangled and fell, onto the white bedspread.

'Oh – oh, I don't know.' For all my medication I had nothing suitable. I handed him tissues and a toothmug of water which he spilled everywhere. I wondered about offering him a mouthwash as cough mixture, but they all had 'Not to be Swallowed' on the labels. 'No I can't see anything – I've no sweets or anything.' I was on my knees under the basin, delving into my sponge-bag, when the situation struck me as ludicrous. I stood up and bent over him so abruptly that he cowered. I hit him three resounding smacks on the back, losing aim somewhat with the last.

'There. That should cure you.'

He couldn't reply for having to catch his breath. The wheezing coming from his chest was quite alarming.

'Look, you must go now. I'm sorry, but you must, you just absolutely must.'

His heaving gradually subsided and I hovered impatiently over him. But he was slumped and looked utterly worn out and there were long pauses between each short, heavy breath it seemed such an effort to take. His eyes were closed.

'Look, I'm not standing for any more of this. Either you go now, or I rouse the hotel.'

There was no sign that he heard.

I stood on the bed and lifted him by the armpits from behind. But it was impossible to get a grip. He had gone limp, and simply collapsed backwards against my knees.

'Do you want me to get you an ambulance?' I asked sarcastically, in sheer irritation.

'Yes please.'

'It's the police you'll get if anyone,' I told him contrarily, provoked by my helplessness to a vicious mutter. I stood over him, watching the filthy fingers twitch, swollen, curling, like so many poisoned slugs on the bed-clothes.

I was the last person on earth who had any right to feel such physical revulsion.

I could go and find another room, or sleep in the foyer even. He would only follow, I thought in despair; he wasn't really asleep. But it was worth a try. I tiptoed backwards towards the door. It was as though I had strings attached to me that hauled up his torso. He surveyed me with his little eyes, blinking rapidly, solemn as a child that has been suddenly awoken and beholds a miracle.

'Woman, woman. . . what is your name?'

'I haven't got one. Now get out.'

I would have to do something. Perhaps I should set off the fire alarm. But calling the police might, in the end, create less consternation. How was I to let them in though?

'Not got one? Not got one?' He was talking as though soothing an underprivileged child and I thought: surely I ought to be able to bundle him out of the window. Surely. I wasn't feeling drunk any more.

'That's right. I don't really exist. . .'

I grasped the lapels of his jacket, not remembering they would be wet and slimy from his slobbering. He grabbed my elbows, pulling me on top of him with a kind of cackle as we fell back, and I felt his legs knot around me. My arms were buckled under me against his chest and I found I couldn't lever myself out of his

69

embrace. I turned my head aside to avoid his stinking breath and he bit hard into my ear.

'Help. Help. Help. Help.' Now that I'd started – now that there was no way of pretending nothing was happening, I might as well go on. 'Help. Help. Help.' The arms clamped me more and more tightly, obviously in an effort to smother me. 'Help. Help. Help. Help.' Suddenly I was on the ground and he was scrambling all over me to get to the window. When it struck me I was going to be found shouting on the floor, perfectly safe and entirely alone, I stopped.

Out on the fire-escape, the old man stopped too, listening in the silence of the night. There was nothing to suggest I had been heard, nothing. I held my breath and slowly, all the while listening, he eased his way back into the room. The pin-pricks of his eyes were grim; his face was set. All that moved there was the green snot that bulged in a bubble from his nostril and withdrew, bulged again and withdrew, and again, and again. I could hear the bubbling of it over the laboured sound of his breathing. I had never seen anyone look so vengeful. He had no bottom teeth, but his top teeth had slipped, so that he seemed to be baring them.

He came at me, slowly still, with his arms bent, like a doll's arms, and his fingers bent like claws. I could not scream but a capsule of cold fluid burst in my brain as the tumour had burst in my mouth, and I snatched up the bottles of mouthwashes on the basin and hurled them one after the other and one was glass and smashed on his forehead and made the blood run over his eyes, and I was knocked from behind as the door opened.

It was not the manager, it was Aled.

He didn't speak, or do anything, he just stood there.

It would be just as well if the curtains were as plastic as they looked – the blood could just be wiped off.

Aled drew handfuls of tissues from the box by the bed and took the farmer's hands away from his face. He ignored the broken glass scrunching under his feet, and the old man's groans, and made him sit down, and dabbed gently and rhythmically at that ugly little face, patting softly, looking intently, and patting again. Saying nothing.

70

There seemed to be just the one cut, on what had once been his hairline, but it was long and tending to gape.

Aled spoke to him resignedly: he might have been telling him he'd live.

The old slack face suddenly trembled with anger again, making the blood well up faster: he pointed a shaking, righteous finger at me, and let rip in Welsh.

Aled sought to calm him: they used the one English word to each other, 'assault'. I began to get frightened. Aled was the only witness and he was in cahoots with the old man over some kind of illegal bartering (whatever was Ceri's 'fertilizer' a euphemism for, I wondered?). In this part of Wales, what chance would I stand in court? And all I had come there for was to wait. . .

I suddenly thought: I'm going to be sick, and I wanted water, so I wrenched frantically at the tap, but it would not turn. I felt Aled hold me up and lead me to the bed and press the back of my neck, till I couldn't breathe with my head in my skirt, and when I lifted it, the old man had gone.

I was lying on the bed and Aled was crouching, sweeping the glass into a dustpan. He must have heard me stir, for he looked up, grunted, and went back to sweeping. He was going about it quite meticulously.

'What did he say?'

'Pardon?'

'What did he say?'

'Oh – he didn't apologise, if that's what you mean.'

'I suppose I'm to be sued for assault now,' I said bitterly.

'Oh I hardly think so,' he assured me casually, standing up, preoccupied with looking round for slivers of glass he might have missed. 'Still,' he mused, his consoling tone laced with a mild, vague irony, 'one would hardly have thought all that was quite necessary, somehow. . .'

'What do you know about it? Walking in when it was all over! If you'd come when you were needed it wouldn't have happened.' Then the full irony of his criticism of my actions hit me. 'And you're a fine one to talk, aren't you? You looked ready enough to use violence yourself the first time I saw you. And that was in the middle of a field, in the middle of the day, not in the middle of your bedroom in the middle of the night. And I didn't have any sexual designs on you either, I'll have you know.'

He looked as if he might be suppressing a grin. 'I didn't throw it, though. . .' he pointed out.

'No – I got out of the way before you could.'

'Come on – I've just rescued you.'

'Me? Oh? I thought it was him you were rescuing.'

'Well. . . he did seem to be rather more in need of it than you, it's true. . .'

'Yes, he gives a good impression of needing rescuing doesn't he?' I said sarcastically, remembering how I had dragged him into the room. 'I keep trying to rescue him from you, and you keep trying to rescue him from me.'

Aled can't have known what I was talking about, but he said, rather stonily now: 'It's hard to see what harm a doddering old man like that could do you.'

'More harm than he could do you anyway,' I said steadily, hoping to convey to Aled my criticism of him – of the way he and the others had hounded the old man in the Hungry Cheese when he wasn't even threatening them. Aled blushed and turned away, but I still couldn't be sure he had read my remark aright.

'Then the more glad you should be to be rescued.'

'Oh yes – by the very person who caused it all. Well if it's gratitude you want, thanks.' I was being unreasonable, I knew; the clashing relief and resentment had got hopelessly out of control.

'Caused it all? What are you on about?'

'You know perfectly well what I'm on about. If it hadn't been for you lot pestering him down in the Hungry Cheese he wouldn't have come up here looking for someone to take it out on.' I felt a sense of shame rising. 'Just like I'm taking it out on you now,' I conceded. 'Full circle.'

When he laughed, however, I became more incensed than ever.

'Heaven knows what kind of bribery and corruption was going on down there, negotiating over "fertilizer", whatever nonsense that might be, but you and your talk of fertilizer certainly gave him ideas.'

I waited for a dry comment about someone my age being an unlikely choice in that direction, but it didn't come. Nothing did. He was staring at me blankly, with cruel eyes, his long arms dangling, and I cursed myself for perhaps getting Ceri into trouble.

'He wouldn't stop muttering about the price of fertilizer,' I scolded, hoping to suggest I'd heard the term from the old man.

I felt increasingly uneasy under Aled's continuing, unchanging gaze.

'And if you imagine you're going to chum up with him and get your own back by having me up for assault, let me tell you I shan't hesitate to mention your prison record.'

I couldn't believe what a fool I was being, but all he said was: 'Do you know what I was in prison for?' I could hardly catch the words, they were so low.

'No and I don't want to,' I snapped, flopping into the only chair, as though the conversation was at an end.

'Well you're going to know.' He came towards me and leant forward to hold the arms of the chair, pinning me in it. His young clean fingers, their nails bitten to the quick, were white with tension. 'I got nine months for being in known possession of stolen goods.' He spoke disjointedly, searching for words. 'And do you know what those stolen goods were? A road-sign – an English road-sign. . . removed from Trefechan bridge during a peaceful demonstration by people who thought they should have a right to use their own language in their own country. "Give way". It was being passed round when the police pounced. I pleaded guilty.' He spoke with carefully modulated sarcasm, but with such effort he was almost out of breath. His mouth was only just under control.

'And now I suppose I'm going to have as much trouble with you as with the old man,' I said spitefully, and he left.

CHAPTER SIX

The flood in the back yard of the hotel subsided. I took it the drains had been unblocked, but it may simply have been that it rained less persistently; all I knew was that I no longer lay listening to the milkman or the delivery men swashing wearily through water. Instead they trailed gumboots, miserably too big for them, through resisting weeds, and across scrapers that laced the weeds like spiders' webs. There was, I discovered, quite a network of these scrapers, linking the four corners of the yard, as if to draw whatever creatures tumbled down the fire-escapes to the tangled knot of intersections at the centre. They had been laid, I suppose, as tramlines through the puddles, or as traps for trespassers (for they squawked edgily as knife-blades under the most innocuous footfall).

From where the water had receded, there were stains – lines of scum around the walls, as around the rim of a drain. And against the walls were washed little piles of weeds; the weakest weeds, obviously, though even the sturdiest, that had penetrated the flood, now lay flat and bedraggled and half smashed to pulp. It was a ravaged place. Not a single stem retained any sign of the strength with which its young shoot had once cracked open the tarmac of the yard. Now, after sprouting like an army from the earth, they were fit for nothing but to clutch like beggars at the ankles of passing tradesmen.

The frogs had been left high and dry of course. And yet I couldn't see how it could possibly have been the evaporation, or draining away, of the pool, that accounted for the carpet of little green corpses. Some of them seemed to have been stamped on; they lay prostrate, with splayed limbs, flat as cast-off skins. Others were shrivelled and mangled, as though they had been hammered against the walls, the way squid are killed. Perhaps, without water, they had no refuge from the cats, which had started teasing them playfully with their claws in, and then with their claws out, sadistically, roused by the helpless terror of the tiny animals. Or perhaps it was crows that massacred them, for crows were everywhere – crouching on the rooftops, pecking irritably at debris in the gutters, or cawing down tunnels of chimneys, where the coarse noise was magnified to the ghostly, gloating cackle that often broke out down in the Hungry Cheese.

I couldn't bear to think of Aled, I was so ashamed of the way I had behaved towards him; but I was vexed with him, too, and with the old man, nearly as much as with myself. All kinds of pettiness had broken loose between us, ripping up the strait-jacket of my numbness and my pain, and seizing possession of me like devils, and I didn't care to remember it.

So I avoided the Hungry Cheese. I spent the evenings in my room, like some senseless lover with a host of ladders pitched to the balcony. But all that appeared, in the wake of the frogs, were rats; and whether the cats could not catch them, or the crows gave them a wide berth, or what, I don't know, but they thrived, and in the end I could hardly stand the sight of them there below me in the yard. Sometimes, I swear, I caught them feeding on one another; and sometimes, when I was woken at night by the stealthy metallic whispers of the scrapers, I would look down not upon suitors but upon a dozen rats cavorting, their naked tails squirming like snakes – and gleaming, if there was moonlight.

In madder moments they would go tearing up the struts at the end of the banisters where the fire-escapes ended in the yard, but they never got far before dropping off. I would hear the soft plops they made as they toppled to the ground. Then, one evening, I saw a big one, on the balcony of the floor below, gingerly creeping, one foot at a time, along the top of the handrail.

I tried television, watching alone in a vast lounge, but the world outside had grown too extraordinary to be taken in by. Everything had changed – actors sounded like mouthpieces, so did newsreaders, so did reporters. Nothing rang true. I had lost touch with the conventions of reality, I suppose, and watched like something buried in the bowels of the earth.

Someone else soon noticed the rats, and they went the way of the others down at the river. There was a low scraping sound in the yard one day, an ominously slow sound, and there on the metal blades lay a rat, looking for all the world as though he had lost his footing on ice. The little paws were galvanised into a frenzy, flapping either side of him like the oars of a boat at the brink of a weir. But it was hopeless: the body they strove to propel was a ton weight, quite beyond his failing strength. For a moment I thought that on top of everything, he was losing the entrails from his abdomen, but all I had seen was his tail. I looked at my watch; I would just be in time for a drink, if I hurried.

After that, my old routine established itself, and I was back in the Hungry Cheese whenever it was open. Ceri, though he never asked where I'd been, eagerly fixed a time for us to play pool in the junk-room, as though to catch me before I disappeared again. Back on the whisky, I listened in a sleepy way to the noises of the bar and let the red and black shapes float in front of my eyes, feeling myself grow weightless with them. I didn't care twopence that the picture only became more and more amorphous. I no longer expected, or even hoped, to see what had amazed and excited Ceri, or what Aled had observed with indifference.

When the policeman came in, I knew he was alien without turning to look. His stride gave him away; it was purposeful. He belonged, not to our lunch-time gloom, but to the harsh hole of sunlight at the top of the steps – to the glare that seemed to be trying to sidle in with him. All movement, and all sound, save for his own, were arrested. All eyes, save for mine, were on him; I watched Thomas watching what was held in the outstretched hand coming towards him.

As he followed the policeman out, Thomas paused to ask if I would look after the bar for a few minutes. He seemed vague, rather than agitated, and he took my corresponding blankness for assent. I thought: well I won't bother to move anyhow; but Thomas was back holding up the hinged section of the bar for me to pass through.

He was not back in a few minutes.

There were three old men there who gave no sign of having seen anything amiss.

My only other customers were Ceri and his mates, and them I ignored.

After a while I even plucked up the courage to cross over to the hearth and retrieve my whisky.

But on my return I was followed: there were wolf-whistles: I was crowded and jostled and almost prevented from squeezing behind the bar. And when I did get there, they leaned over the bar at me, crushing one another, savouring the menace of their heavy-metal advance, smirking, pestering like bullocks over a fence.

But they were, in truth, a scrawny lot – the weak stock produced by in-breeding, or over-breeding, or by war. It might be what one generation always makes of the next. All through my own youth, after all, dentists had wanted to know whether I had been born in the war. (It wasn't what dentists said when they saw the inside of my mouth nowadays.)

They settled into poses with their beers, staring insolently from their lop-sided heads, daring me to find a rule they would not break or a line they would not cross.

I wished Aled would walk in.

I must have been in pretty bad shape to see salvation in Aled.

Oh, what the hell. Let them raid the bar. It was nothing to me what they did.

Even Ceri was staring, half apologetic, half defiant, waiting to see how I would react.

'You don't want to get too excited,' I told him, 'or all that plumage will uncurl with the static you're building up.' One of them laughed, but Ceri looked down, blushing slightly I fancied, and the others transferred their stares to him, challenging him now. The lad alongside him said something in an undertone of disgust.

I was sorry. I shouldn't have picked on him. It was the age-old habit I had despised in teachers of isolating the weakest in any group of rebels. But I was rusty, and there could be a fuss if they smashed the place up. (Not that Thomas would be likely to invoke the law, if the brief impression I had got of his relations with it was anything to go by.)

Ceri turned away, and I didn't know what I could do to prevent his resentment. I might have tried something – anything – but a boy with a gilt razor-blade hanging from one ear was demanding attention. With his head tilted so far it seemed dislocated by the weight of the adornment, he was looking at a label above my head and pronouncing the syllables of 'Tia Maria' like a child learning to read. 'Tia Maria. Get me a Tia Maria,' he insisted, adding '*os gwelwch yn dda,*' with ironic ingratiating politeness and something of a bow, in which he affected to hit his head comically on the bar.

Instinctively I looked round for a stool, and there was laughter, not all of it unkind. Without thinking, I lifted the hinged flap of the bar (conscious for a second of the way they drew back), grasped the sulking Ceri by the wrist and pulled him in with me. He looked taken aback, and then rather sheepish as his mates cheered. Too late I saw how horribly misguided I had been in thinking I could redeem my humiliation of Ceri by favouring him – I was simply compounding the humiliation by using him to get me out of an embarrassment.

I also thought, likewise too late, that it might have been a mistake to infringe the barrier of the bar.

To the others' mocking, rhythmic thumping, Ceri reached above me and handed me the bottle. Then he ducked back out into the world he knew about.

The bully I served stared contemptuously at me while he picked up the glass, downed it in one, grimaced, and did not pay. (Just as well – I had no idea of the cost.)

With pathetic imitation his friends wanted Cointreau, Southern Comfort, Creme de Menthe. Ceri, perhaps smarting, or perhaps evading further enlistment, had wandered over to the hearth. I refused to serve anyone until the Tia Maria had been paid for.

The demands became more extravagant, and then turned personal. But the more shocking the words, the less aggressive became their manner, and the most lewd suggestions were called out over their shoulders to me as they turned back to the dartboard in disgruntled boredom.

I became worried about Thomas's long absence.

Ceri had refused to rejoin the game. He was on the settle where

I usually sat, balancing sideways on it, supporting his pint on his knees that were drawn up almost to his chin, and rolling his forehead against the glass as if for coolness. He looked up when two of his pals, who had long been conspiring, slunk across to me, their hands smugly behind their backs.

They parted like stalking cats, to approach me obliquely, and then all hell broke loose. Shooting, they're shooting, I thought. Glass shattered around my ears as one after another the bullets came at me. But they were only throwing darts – picking off choice portions of my anatomy in the mirrors behind me, I supposed, since they would never have missed had they been out to get me.

After the bust-up, the two of them stood in amazement, their spent arms dangling like broken limbs. One was the youth I had served with Tia Maria. 'Cool, man, cool,' he said, his head cocked now in a kind of curious acknowledgement.

I did not feel cool, I felt contempt. What on earth did they suppose those silly little winged missiles and bits of broken glass amounted to, when there was a time-bomb ticking away inside me?

Not one of the gang stirred. But the three old men did: they gasped and got up and started fussing, appalled.

The two youths seemed to share my own intolerance of fuss. They made off, leaving the others to traipse out after them, bearing their black jackets like trophies. All except Ceri. He sat on, brooding as usual, alone and ignored, and eventually there was only me and him left there.

But oh dear, I had not bargained for the aftermath. Back in my room, the moment the door closed, the familiar helpless frustration swamped me like some phobia. I was not a whit less vulnerable to it than when I had first succumbed, that day in the underground, not half an hour after leaving the hospital, when I had burst into tears on the Piccadilly Line – not because of what I had just been told, but because I wanted to go north and the platforms were labelled 'eastbound' and 'westbound'. Now I couldn't face the possibility of meeting anyone, nor even the thought of catching sight of a rat out of the window, but neither could I stand the walls of my room.

There was, however, no sign of any rats, and in the end I sat at the window, on into the evening and on into the night (while the Hungry Cheese opened again and closed), imprisoned behind the bars of the deserted fire-escapes, and, finally, behind the slanting shadows of them too, cast by the moon. There was no movement at all – not of people, not of rats – not even of clouds. Only, I suppose, the moving of the shadows as the moon and the earth revolved.

It is a harsh light, moonlight; far more harsh than the light of the sun – for the shadows it makes are not coloured, as the shadows of sunlight are, but impenetrably black.

In daylight, there are always limits to things – recognisable, reassuring limits. From the moment you open your eyes, whatever you face has shape and size and colour, and you can look away and then look back and it won't have changed. And any human being will have the same way of moving, no matter if they move to the ends of the earth, and the same face, no matter what the expression on it, and the same voice, no matter what it says. But when you close your eyes, and the dark takes over, there are no safeguards of this sort. To nightmare, there are no limits of any sort. . .

'Stop panicking. You're OK. You were dreaming, that's all. You're OK now – just a dream.' Aled, cold with hate, letting go abruptly of my shoulders.

'What's the matter? What's happening?' I was in my own room, but very hampered by the sheets, and damp, and unpleasant. 'What happened?'

'I told you – you were dreaming.'

'But what are you doing here?' He had got up and was standing with his back to me.

'You were screaming, so I came down.'

'No I wasn't.' He held my toothmug, full of water, out to me, his hand dripping all over the blankets, saying nothing. 'No I wasn't.'

'Have it your own way. Do you want this?'

'Who else heard me?' I couldn't bear the thought of another

fuss; and if there was going to be one, I'd better get dressed, quick.

'Look, do you want this or don't you?'

'I want you to go away so that I can get up.' I over-enunciated in sheer exasperation.

'Will you stop panicking. It's only two o'clock and if any mob was thinking of arriving, it would have turned up by now.'

'Mobs are notoriously unreliable,' I grumbled, but I took the water. 'I could do with something stronger than this.'

Aled relaxed a bit and sat at the bottom of the bed, round-shouldered and sad, and when I handed him back the mug, he absently sat drinking the rest of the water. But he can't have been as far away as I thought, for he said, out of the blue: 'You should stop tormenting yourself about it now, you know. It's finished and done with, and in any case it wasn't real.' He spoke in a dismal monotone, gazing into the mug, as though he had been testing a microphone.

I leaned forward to touch one of his grated fingertips. 'I see no sign that you follow your own advice.'

I saw no sign, either, that he understood me.

All I wanted to do was sit still, and be quiet, and keep myself awake, and Aled didn't seem in the mood for talking either; but you can't just keep on saying nothing, with somebody else sitting on the end of the bed.

'I was on this machine – lying on it – tied down.'

Aled put the mug back on the basin, rousing himself as though all his limbs were heavy and aching. 'What machine?'

'Actually, it was the xerox machine we had where I used to teach,' I said in surprise, suddenly able to identify it. 'X-raying me.'

'What happened?'

'People were leaning over me with masks on, peering. The masks moved in and out when they breathed. They were doctors – but underneath they were Ceri Griff and all the others.'

'I wondered if it had anything to do with this afternoon,' said Aled simply.

'They told me that only my bones were left alive. Isn't it funny,' I mused flippantly, 'the way people say "I feel it in my bones"

81

when really that's the only place nobody ever feels anything?' I had known nothing all the while the tumour was eating its way out through my lower jaw and through my cheekbone and through the socket into my skull; only when it set to work demolishing my flesh had I suspected there was anything wrong at all, and then the feeling in my face had gone dead. 'How did you know about this afternoon?'

'It wouldn't have happened if I'd been there.' It was not a boast, it was a fact stated quite humbly, even regretfully, but I reacted very coldly.

'Possibly. But you weren't.'

He pulled himself up a bit as though to nerve himself to look at me.

'What made you scream?' He got off the bed and flopped in the wicker chair, facing me, leaning back with his head resting on his fist, ready to listen. Had he been up when I had screamed, or had he dressed before coming to find out what was going on?

'They started pumping plaster-of-Paris into my bones and that pushed all the marrow out so they had to fix tubes to drain it from my fingers and toes, and they took off their masks to promise me my bones would be stronger than ever though they would never heal.' I stopped the rapid, vicious flow and concluded with a leisurely apathy: 'That was when I must have started struggling – I remember begging them to stop, and them tossing me in a blanket to get the plaster-of-Paris spread evenly through me. Only I expect that was you shaking me really.'

In the silence that fell, I gave in to the feeling of recuperation, drifting into the calm of weakness, knowing I had only to sit still to recover. Thinking how pleasant it was, recovery after suffering that has only been pretend.

After a while Aled asked: 'Are you ill?' He was watching his hand tracing the patterns of the dye in his jeans, as though it was acting quite independently of him.

'How do you mean?'

He looked up innocently, as if to say he had only meant: don't you feel well? Then he frowned in the preoccupied way he had, and started pulling at broken ends of wicker in the arm of the

82

chair and letting them snap back. 'I was just wondering what you were doing here.'

'Funny how you all want to know that. All except the one man I might reasonably expect to want to know.'

Aled grinned: 'Oh, Thomas is an old ostrich, you know. And a coward,' he added more seriously, still twanging the wicker-work.

'It's as well for you he is, isn't it?'

'What do you mean?' It was his turn to be sharp now, but I wasn't really sure what I had meant.

'Well, think of what he might have said to that policeman if he'd been less of an ostrich and coward,' I bluffed.

'What did he say to you when he saw the state of the bar afterwards?' was all Aled's response.

'To me, nothing. He told the Almighty they didn't know what they were doing.'

'How Christ-like!' Aled leaned back and closed his eyes.

'Oh, I don't think he was implying they should be forgiven.' My primness got no reaction. 'He also muttered something about not knowing where it would all lead.'

'What did you say?'

'Told him there was no knowing in this place where anything was going to lead, even the corridors.' It was a lie – I had thought it, but I had said nothing.

His head lay tilted over the top of the chair, in repose. Only the wicker-work flicking under his fingers betrayed his restlessness.

'I wish you wouldn't do that.'

I felt surprise, and guilt, when his fingers obeyed: he seemed altogether at peace now. But I didn't want him to go to sleep there.

'If you really want to know, I'm here because I'm waiting to have a tumour removed.'

I waited for him to stay stretched out, indifferent; or sit up, embarrassed; or retreat as though I were infectious. But he did none of those things. He lifted his head, gravely, showing no surprise and no concern, but just. . . well. . . just conveying a sense of respect I suppose. He asked whether it was malignant.

'I didn't think to enquire.'

Still no surprise, he simply went on to ask other things.

It was strange to hear the consultant's words repeated aloud for the first time.

Even stranger to hear myself confessing fears I was only half aware had taken root.

They were quickly said. The starvation of the long silence I had been living in was hardly assuaged at all.

Aled picked up the hospital's phrases that I threw out with clipped offhandedness – 'tendency to recur', 'bone-grafting' – picked them all up and sorted them out, methodically, calmly.

I was reluctantly grateful, and humble in face of his carefulness of me; but humiliated, somehow, by having everything taken out of my preserve and made order of.

Suddenly, I wanted him to lapse into brutal unconcern or to dissolve into pity – it didn't matter which. Anything to break the control of that moderate considering.

It was my own control that snapped of course. At his verdict that I was lucky they could operate, I turned on him. 'Lucky? You think I'm lucky? You think I'm lucky? You think I'm lucky?'

He was leaning forward with his elbows on his knees and his hands clasped, and he looked up slowly, infuriatingly, as though half-deaf. 'Yes,' he answered, evenly, as though it took him courage to say so. 'So many people have nothing at all to hope for.'

'Are you talking about yourself?' I asked cattily, mocking his permanently dejected air.

He looked steadily back, hostile for a second, but the pale mouth stayed shut. He straightened, till his hands, not his elbows, rested on his knees, his fingers inward, their eaten ends concealed. He seemed to be on the point of standing up. But he surveyed the room first.

'Well, thank you for explaining why you came here,' he said, in such bewilderment that I laughed. He smiled back. His eyes should have been blue under all that fair hair but they weren't, they were grey – not even a greenish-grey like the sea, but a stale grey, like overcast skies.

'I was trying to commune with nature, but you soon put a stop to that.'

The corners of his mouth turned down in wry apology. 'You must be glad you came.'

'Oh, I don't know. At least I've got away from the people who had to keep harping on about cancer, and the ones who were scared to mention it.'

'You're very intolerant.'

'Aren't you?'

'No – not in that personal way.'

'Seemed pretty personal to me when you were ranting and raving and throwing stones.'

He was drawing out the white hairs on one of his bare arms, concentrating, as though he had found a tick embedded there. 'You do bear a grudge, don't you?'

'Nearly bore a scar didn't I?'

'No.'

'And all because I was looking at a wreath among some Abbey ruins.' He remained impassive, aware that I was fishing. 'What is that wreath all about then?' I asked impulsively.

He looked puzzled, and I thought he was going to say: 'What wreath?', but it was my train of thought that confused him. 'That? That's to commemorate Llywelyn ap Gruffudd – he's buried there, seven hundred years this year.'

That long, since the conquest of Wales.

Well, since our ancestors had run amok together on the bridge at Builth, or had stood together in servility a little while later under the battlements of Caernarfon Castle and received at the hands of the conqueror his new-born heir who did not discriminate between the two languages, we had been divided. While Aled had learnt to look on Llywelyn as the last Prince of Wales, I had been taught to see his successor, Edward, as the first.

'And which version did you teach?' was Aled's only comment.

But I hadn't taught history.

'It's funny about Llywelyn isn't it?' I was so tired suddenly, I had to lie down, but I curled up tight, so that Aled shouldn't feel obliged to move his feet from the end of the bed.

'What's funny?'

'The way his assassin didn't recognise who he'd killed. I like that, that Llywelyn was indistinguishable from his men.'

'Why?'

'I don't know, I just do.' I had had my fill of people using all kinds of posturing to assert their authority by. I had been up to the eyeballs in it during the fight for power at the amalgamation of the two schools, in which I had come a cropper.

Aled received all this with his eyes closed, and only my conviction that he was asleep made me give vent to my bitterness. I was taken aback when he responded. 'So,' he said with equally bitter irony and his eyes still shut, 'Sounds like he's your hero, Llywelyn.'

I was so astonished by his tone I could say nothing.

'You can, of course, on the other hand, interpret his undistinguished clothing as a disguise – an obvious way of remaining inconspicuous.'

'Oh obvious! It only got him killed!'

'Or he might have been trying to keep a secret assignation with a woman, as was rumoured at the time.'

That was beneath contempt. Llywelyn's wife had just died at the birth of their only child.

'But what he was really up to, most likely, was spying. Underhandedly assessing the degree of support for himself among the locals. Disguised, so they would be deceived into betraying themselves.'

'I thought he'd have been your hero,' was all I could think of to say, feebly, childishly.

'He is.'

For a moment I was frightened; about what he might be up to, over in the caravans, here in the hotel; about what he was leading the others into, down in the Hungry Cheese; about the hold he had over the gormless Ceri. But his severity melted into sadness as he mused on: 'The country was lost by mistake, by accident, trivially, an insignificant murder in a wood. . .'

'And is that how it is to be regained, too?'

But to that he would say nothing. I suppose that neither of us, at three in the morning, in the sweaty and airless room, had the strength to put much faith in Wales. But at three in the morning, too, we could mourn as if waiting for the second coming. Of

Arthur. He, perhaps, would be neutral between us – for he would maybe speak neither in the tongue of the conquered, like Aled, nor in the tongue of occupation, like me, but in the dead language of previous conquerors, whom we had long long ago forgiven and forgotten.

The night was without wind and without rain, and so silent we heard a distant clock chime three – faint, peaceful. The grandfather clock in the lobby probably, even though it was not going. . . Aled snuggled down, turning sideways, resting his cheek on the palm of his hand. I noticed how broad his hands were, compared with the rest of him. But the nails on them were not just bitten, they were tiny, as though they had been savaged from early childhood and had never stood a chance.

Then we must have dozed.

I half heard him asking something.

'Pardon?'

'Are you in pain?'

'No. Why? Are you?'

'You were groaning.'

'Oh. I'm sorry.'

'I can't see any reason for being sorry.'

'I expect I woke you.'

'I don't expect you did.' A sleepy smile, around the deep brown bags below his eyes.

'It's nearly always aching. The tumour burst into my mouth when I had a wisdom tooth extracted, so there's a hole there. But it only gets really bad when I eat.' I hoped he would not make the logical jump to the fact that it got bad when I talked, too.

'Best at night, then,' he said encouragingly, and smiled again, into my eyes. Without looking away, his eyes closed.

He settled, already dropping off, stretching his arms towards me over the arm of the chair. The fingers he seemed to strive to keep concealed lay unconsciously exposed: because I had never seen him smoke, I was surprised to see the yellow stains on them.

It was disturbing, such unguardedness from so guarded a man. They reached out, long white skinny arms, in mute appeal, one wrist across the other, as though he bared them meekly for the

87

handcuffs to be fixed. Had he gone that meekly, I wondered, when he had been arrested on the bridge? Probably. Probably.

He must watch the state of the language like I watched the state of my jaw, noticing here a little improvement, there an alarming set-back, and pledging himself to make more effort. For an unhealthy language, like an unhealthy body, needed to be watched and cossetted and self-consciously cared for.

In repose his face looked angular and ill, save for his lips – their delicate, unusual pallor was not of sickness. Even so, it was a sick room we were in – a smell of sickness seemed to hang heavily there, and everything about me was greasy and damp, my face, my hair, my hands.

Aled rolled over onto his back, flexing his shoulders as if they were stiff. He was fortunate in his eyebrows – they kept his hair out of his eyes; white below the blond fringe, they looked like age blocking the way of youth.

'I suppose to you I am a fanatic,' he said. I turned away, embarrassed at having been caught staring.

'Then you must be more conscious of being so than I am.'

He snorted. 'For people like you there is simply no middle ground between being an extremist and giving up your inheritance, is there? Is there?'

It was the last thing I felt like talking about, but I wasn't going to be pressurised by his insistence. 'Well. Is it so evil to tolerate abuse rather than object to it? In a supposedly Christian country,' I added lamely.

Aled sat up to gaze at me incredulously.

'Such people are slaves.' The rhetoric was unbearably wearying. It reminded me how young he was.

'Yes I suppose they are.'

But Aled continued to gaze in the same way.

'I suppose your people are such people,' he said slowly.

'Certainly they were. And there are a lot like them. It's surprising how many people survive by lying low. Not that I'm doing too well myself on that score, mind you. And I have rather gone off my inheritance just now, too – it was hardly a very tactful thing for you to appeal to.' But my bitterness was utterly self-indulgent – I hadn't the foggiest whether one inherited a tendency towards ameloblastomas or not. Aled disregarded the lapse into self-pity, however.

'Lying low is all very well for a while. But there comes a time when defencelessness means death.'

'Certainly there does.' I was weary beyond.

Aled had taken a box of matches from his pocket; he smirked now as he caught sight of the 'England's Glory' label. Almost absently he extracted a match and struck it. It flared up, its flame reflected in the intertwining canes of the chair. I thought: my God, it was my defencelessness he was on about, not his own, and I suddenly found, Christian country or no, that I wasn't going to just sit there while he set fire to the bedclothes around me. But I was still horribly enmeshed in them, and as I scrambled to free myself the match burned away till it touched his fingers – then he took its dying head in his other hand and upended it so that the flame crept up the whole length of the sliver of wood and then shrank away. He put the little black stalk back into the box, took out a fresh match, and did the same again.

So that was how he got all those little yellow scorch-marks on his fingers.

'We are all slaves,' I told him. 'Just look at us. There's Ceri, tied to his mother and tied to you. . .'

'He's not tied to me.'

'Yes he is – you're tied to the people you hero-worship. And then there's you – slave to your nationalism; and Thomas, who's pretty well slave to everyone; and me, slave to this wretched tumour.' I watched him as he lay blinking at the ceiling; then I lay back and contemplated the ceiling too. 'I expect that's the way you think of me,' I said more quietly. 'As a tumour – a painful presence, threatening you. The enemy in your midst. The native who has betrayed the culture and the language. There's nothing more subversive.'

He seemed to consider this for a while, and when he spoke it was so gently I was misled for a second into thinking he was saying something quite unconnected. 'No, that isn't the way I think of you, Ann. We come out of your past, us lot – but you sit there at the fender in the Hungry Cheese like our future.'

'Then I'm the luckier,' I retorted. 'You might fill me with regret, but I must fill you with despair.'

'Maybe.'

'And yet you go on optimistically slapping green paint over place-names,' I said, probing rather, but desperately hoping that *was* the kind of thing he was doing.

'"I should remain committed to Wales even if I was certain that within ten years Wales would be finished,"' he quoted. 'Saunders Lewis.'

'Who, as I remember, said it was alright for blood to flow as long as it was Welsh blood and not English,' I remarked sarcastically, raising myself on my elbows to watch his reaction. 'Now there's a slave for you.'

'Whatever I'm slave to, it's not Saunders Lewis,' he said coldly, leaving me unclear as to whether he eschewed bloodshed altogether, or simply wanted no racial discrimination in it.

Why was he sitting on there, through the night, talking to me? Was it because he saw, in me, the descendants who would no longer talk in the same tongue or read his books or sing his songs or share his ideas or beliefs, but whose connection with him was betrayed, perhaps, by an unusual word or expression here and there, the origins of which had been lost sight of?

'I don't think you should look on the future so bleakly as to see me heralding it,' I told him. 'The fate of a nation can change surprisingly sometimes. World opinion is pretty fickle.'

'Easy for you – that attitude. "Terrorists" must have been everywhere when you were young – Malaya, Kenya, Israel, everywhere. And then one day the word would disappear from the news headlines, I suppose, and the head of a new independent state would arrive in London to meet the Queen. Well, not any longer. Those expedient changes of heart are gone. "Terrorists" remain "terrorists" now, year in, year out, whether they're Irish, Palestinian, Basque or whatever.'

He made me conscious, only, of how remote from the world I felt, trapped in my sick-room, at the heart of interminable corridors and bays and niches and doors and dead-ends.

90

'Don't get so het up. It's true I get scared sometimes, by all the gallivanting that goes on out there on the fire-escape, but I would hardly call it terrorism.' I was probing again.

'We're not on it that much.'

'Not much you're not. It gets like that Martin Escher picture out there – *Ascending and descending*. You know – the one with masses of people belting up and down staircases, all under the impression they're getting somewhere, when all they're really doing is chasing round in circles.'

'No.' He wasn't remotely interested, but he said: 'You shouldn't get scared.' He asked me whether I had been scared that lunch-time in the Hungry Cheese.

'Not at the dart-throwing. But that wasn't the worst thing that went on in the bar this afternoon.'

'Oh?' He looked across at me, and I saw that Thomas had chosen to say nothing. 'What else happened?'

There was, I well knew, never, in human existence, any release from anything. But at three in the morning, and in the aftermath of nightmare, you can labour under the illusion that there might be.

I began explaining heavily that the way things were, I stood no chance of getting another job, that knowing this I had sold the car and tried to hang on to the house, that I had finally been forced to part with that too. But he, of course, doubtlessly being against anyone owning anything, would have no conception of what it was like to lose everything at the onset of middle-age.

'Stop being so bloody defensive.'

'I'm not bloody defensive. I'm bloody poor.' I said it signif-icantly, yet still he didn't seem to understand. But his face was so devoid of expression that I began to wonder if he hadn't guessed for some time.

Then he looked at me straight, and I realised with a pang that he thought I was asking him for money.

'If you're up to roughing it, you can doss down in one of the caravans behind the Abbey if you like. . .'

'I wouldn't dream of touching either of those caravans with a barge-pole. . .'

91

'But it's all I can offer,' he ended, not so much firmly, as despondently.

'I'm not asking you for anything.'

'Well the offer's there anyway.'

'Thank you.' I was left feeling neither grateful nor mollified, just miserable.

When the grandfather clock struck four, it sounded slow and forlorn, and the sound seemed to go dead, as though it was the bell tolling from one of our legendary cities under the sea.

It was Aled who brought the subject up again.

'Ceri Griff was ashamed about it, you know.'

'Ashamed about what?'

'Not stopping the others from attacking you.'

'Ashamed? He has more reason to be angry than ashamed – I humiliated him in front of them.'

'Well, he's ashamed anyway: so you mustn't think of avoiding the Hungry Cheese because of what happened – like last time. OK?' He was the patronising peacemaker dealing with a pair of scrapping kids.

It made me react with an even greater, more airy aloofness. 'Oh, you needn't worry about that. I've got the means to carry on drinking for a while again now.'

This time, it clicked.

There was a pause, and then he said non-committedly: 'So.' I watched him struggle against wanting to know anything more, and lose. 'How much was it you took?'

'I thought it was five tens, but when I counted it, there turned out to be six.' I sounded remorseful, but only about the last tenner.

'Oh well.' He spoke lightly, as though he'd weighed the scales and found in my favour. 'I suppose it's only going to find its way back to where it came from.'

'Does that make it any different?' Then I asked, forgetting: 'Have you ever stolen?'

'I was in prison for stealing a road-sign,' he said as though he hadn't told me before.

'That makes me feel ten times better of course.'

'Stop worrying. Just think of Peredur and feel justified.'

'Think of what?'

'Not what, who. Peredur.'

'Tell me about him.'

Now that Aled knew, the guilt was altered. I was the sinner who, after the false comfort of confession, basks in the advice of the priest. But I was terribly tired.

'When Peredur set out on his quest,' Aled began, rather as though he were telling a bedtime story, and swinging his legs at me over the chair-arm. 'His mother placed three moral obligations upon him. One was to rescue any damsel in distress. . .'

'Oh, is that where you get it from?'

'Shut up. The second was to pray at any chapel he chanced upon. And the third was to consume any food (take drink as read) he found, if he was hungry, even if it was not offered to him. . .'

'Um. Thou shalt not steal. . .' I muttered.

'There are times,' declared Aled as though about to expound his basic philosophy, 'when one is forced to choose between being a Celt and being a Christian.'

'H'm. Whatsisname's mother seemed quite happy to mix them.'

'Whatsisname's mother was a. . .' Like a bleep obliterating an obscene word, the wicker arm over which his legs were slung, gave, with a splintering of bamboo. '. . . woman in a million,' he finished up appreciatively, most of him reduced to the floor.

'Oh God, Aled. It'll take the whole sixty quid for another chair.'

'Yes but Ann, what a way out for your conscience.'

'Oh get out.' I flung the first thing I laid my hands on, which turned out to be my hairbrush. Aled sat on the carpet, ruefully rubbing the side of his head where it had made contact.

'It would have been the pillows,' I apologised, 'if they hadn't gone out the window during a previous incursion into violence.'

Still holding his head, Aled got up and walked straight out of the room, without a glance, without a word. I was filled with a horrible, sinking dismay and went to the door after him, but desperate as I felt, I could not bring myself to shout down the corridor, not even to call out 'goodnight'. Nauseous, aching and exhausted, I went back to bed.

But the door opened and Aled strode in, grinning stupidly, and hugging two pillows. Neither of us said anything, but I sat up to let him stack them behind me, and as he straightened he paused, and touched the diseased side of my face with the back of his hand. He might have been overcoming a revulsion, but he was not offensive – he had the gingerly gentleness of an awestruck child – so I held my breath and didn't react.

But for a long time after he had gone, I lay awake. Outside, it was quiet no more – the birds were beginning to sing. Not the crows that would be the only things cawing later in the day, but blackbirds and thrushes and other birds I could not identify, that seemed to sing in the dawn chorus and then vanish. I lay awake, not soothed by their rare music, but sweating once again.

Whenever I touched my own face, I still had sensation. Not the normal sensation, of course, for it was in my fingertips only, but it was sensation of a sort. But I had watched Aled stretch out his hand and stroke my face, and I had felt nothing. Nothing at all.

I had not known how it would be, for Aled was the only other person who had touched my face in the months since it had become numb.

And so, for all that we had said to each other, and for all the softness of the silences between us, his departing gesture drove me back into my isolation. And instead of Aled, I thought of Llywelyn, whose death had lost us our nationhood, and whose dust lay just across the fields from us. If Aled was to be believed, that was.

CHAPTER SEVEN

Under stress, you make resolves; and then you drift away from them, the way threads of smoke drift from dying flames and dwindle into thin air. When you are made redundant people are constantly warning you, not to let go, to keep a grip of things, to hang on like grim death, and for a while you make an effort. Even a dying flame will lick stubbornly for a while at what it cannot burn. But the pointlessness of struggling, the pointlessness of waking up and then of staying awake, the pointlessness of going to sleep only to wake again, damps down the ardour you summon, until you wonder how anything of it is left, smouldering on underneath, perpetually ready to leap forth, at the least incentive, in another fickle flickering.

The morning after Aled's visit, I began planning again. I would look for a copy of Escher's picture to show him. In the town library. It meant having to join, which (as I was no longer a rate-payer) meant going back to the hotel for Thomas's signature, something he was ridiculously reluctant to part with until I had made a thorough nuisance of myself trailing after him all round the foyer twice, like a stray dog.

Back among the bookshelves I began to suspect there might have been something behind the unusual intensity of his nervousness. For I caught snatches of whispering between the bursts of unseasonal hailstones against the loose panes of the high, frosted windows, and I picked up the English words 'squatters' and 'police', and I saw people pointing towards a rather undistinguished array of books as though they were not books at all but painted spines on a concealed door leading heaven knew where. I thought: whatever's happened, at least Aled wasn't involved, and I imagined myself in court, sole witness to his alibi. I would confess to his staying with me for most of the night, in a charitable endeavour to forestall further nightmares (had that been the truth?), but I might suppress the fact that we had both fallen asleep several times, as being a detail both unhelpful to the cause of justice and open to misinterpretation.

I was idiotically pleased when I lit on a book of prints that contained the perpetually spiralling robots, and I left the building quickly. It had been disconcerting to find how unused I had grown to strangers – so unused, their mere presence was enough, apparently, to bring me out in a sweat. Once in the street I felt calmer, which was odd, as I was among even more strangers there. Perhaps my anxiety in the library had been due, not to people, but to the books – to the medical texts I knew must be stashed away there somewhere: formidable monuments to generation upon generation of terrible suffering, and the even more hideous agonies of the paltry interference of doctors. Had I come across them, I would have passed them by, for I had coldly decided to discover nothing more; but it might have been a resolve in which the muscles of my heart did not have complete faith.

I had thought to show Aled the picture that evening in the Hungry Cheese, but when I got back to the hotel, I wanted him to see it immediately. So I went looking for him, all over the place. The only person I turned up was Ceri. He was playing the machines. When he saw me he looked away and I didn't believe quite enough in Aled's assurance of his shame, to persist and humour him and talk him round. I said only: 'Where's Aled?' and he mumbled something into the gadgetry – it could well have been 'How the fuck should I know?' but he smashed the handles down so violently at the same time, it was virtually inaudible. I could hardly have known those were to be the last words we would exchange (except on the last occasion I ever saw him, when he succumbed to grief) but I feel guilty, even now, of the way I crept away from him that day, leaving him aggressive and troubled and alone in the desecrated dance-hall.

I had lunch and searched again for Aled but he was nowhere. From the road at the back of the hotel I gazed over the empty landscape still choked with the false snow of cotton grass, and I thought I would go back to where I had first come across him, at the Abbey; but I found myself wandering the other way instead, into the town. Under the heavy sun, the tar in the asphalt had turned tacky, almost limpid, and the buildings I passed lay reflected in it. Only where the road shimmered, way ahead of me, was it blank, for the water of mirages casts no reflections.

In the town I could think of nothing better to do than go back to the library, and I slid in as unobtrusively as possible to avoid being offered help.

Dental problems were not a prominent feature, but dictionaries there were in abundance. Crouching, poring over the half intelligible jargon on the spotless pages, I found another sentence to have to learn to live with.

'Ameloblastoma: A locally malignant tumour. . .'

Malignant. So it was malignant. It was malignant, after all. Uncurling like a foetus inside my face, it was malignant. Locally. Only locally, dear God. Chop my head off, I suppose, and I'd be alright. Locally. What the hell did 'locally' mean? Oh God, malignant. Malignant. Oh my dear God.

'Pardon?'

'Are you alright, Mrs?'

I try to explain that I am not married, but the sea has got hold of me and is sucking me down, making confusions, making it difficult for me to hear, and then to see, and then to stand up. . .

Aled did not come drinking that evening, and Thomas had not seen him all day. By closing time, the uncertain spark of contact there had been between us was growing cold, and I wondered how on earth I could have got so worked up about showing him a silly engraving. He would only have given it an offhanded glance, or, if I'd been lucky, frowned at it for a second. Well, maybe that was cynical, but I doubted whether I would have been as gratified by his response to it, as Ceri had been at his response to the picture of the red and black shapes.

That night, I couldn't sleep. I lay on my back staring at the ceiling, not moving, not getting irritable, but just not able to close my eyes. I stared at the ceiling through the long, changing shadows of the moon and long after the moon had gone in; while the stiff curtains stirred and while a light, late-summer shower fell. I stared until the dawn began to break and the air turned grainy around me, like a bad photograph in a cheap newspaper, and shapes of denser grains seemed to form and to float, to float upwards and gather on the ceiling, like a layer of discarded frogspawn-jelly on the surface of a stagnant pond.

Far, far away, somewhere long ago, it was bonfire night.

I half tumbled from the bed, scrambling in panic with the covers. The crackling was real; intimate. The fire-escape. Making for the fire-escape, telling what was solid not by the texture of the greyness so much as by the memory of what had been around me yesterday, and the day before, and the days before that. Scarcely feeling the splinter from the raw wood in the hard roughness of my heel.

Flames. But distant, deceptively distant. Generating their own redness – the sun still buried too deep under the horizon to give colour to the world.

A field of stubble, perhaps?

The wind was fresh, fanning the fire. Sheets of red splashed up like paint on the hillside, spitting sprays of stars into the sky, as if to challenge the order of the cosmos.

Stubble would never blaze like that. Besides, no farmer would even think of setting fire to anything in such a wind.

The crackling sounded so close you half expected to smell the burning and to feel its heat.

In the morning I went back into town. Fine flakes of ash drifted along the streets, listless as winged seeds gliding over ground where there was nowhere to settle. On one corner, a paperboy coughed so despairingly I bought a paper, but I could hear his cough hacking after me again as I followed the smuts to the other end of town.

A terrace of three cottages on the outskirts, gutted. The charred facades stood stubbornly as black teeth; to find its way out the smoke had to weave through the holes where the windows and roofs had been. It was slow, lethargic smoke, not billowing or urgent any more, and the people gathered in the road were no longer urgent either. They hung around half-heartedly, bored but unwilling to leave, as though they feared the shells would flare up again the moment their backs were turned. Only one man looked alert, one of the handful of policemen: he stood stolidly astride, while his colleagues shuffled around him as though the road was too hot for the soles of their feet.

Funny. They were on the front page. Three cottages. Yes, the hillside was right – there they were, on the front page of the paper in my hand. Those very cottages – but intact, as if in a picture that had been taken a hundred years ago.

But it wasn't a hundred years since the Plaid Cymru squatters, stooping to emerge from those doorways, and then stooping even lower to enter the police cars, had been photographed for the *Western Mail*: it was not even a day.

On the way back to my room I bumped into Aled, literally, in one of the corridors. I struggled to compress my paper as he apologised, but he was clearly as preoccupied as I had been, and, thinking he had not recognised me, I stood back to let him pass. But he caught sight of what I had been reading and paused, looking at me, but apparently not quite having the effrontery to ask if he might see the paper.

'I've got that picture to show you,' I said.

He half raised his arm as if to look at his watch and excuse himself, but instead he asked: 'What picture?' I suppose it was the hope he might get a peep at the *Western Mail* that held him.

He lounged as before in my wicker chair, ignoring its broken arm, grinning at the foolish figures tearing around the terrace from which they could never escape. He flicked through a few other prints in the book, then handed it back to me.

'So that's how you see us then.' It was a non-committal comment.

'Well, at times. . . Sometimes you're more like a crowd of hoodlums sneaking onto a derelict helter-skelter in a disused fairground in the dead of night.'

'For kicks.'

'Oh, on that, I don't speculate.'

'You must get quite a view.' He went to the window, as though to assess how much I had seen.

I moved over to stand beside him.

He shook his head: 'Not kids on a helter-skelter.'

'What then?'

'Another kids' thing. I don't know if you'd know it.'

'Oh well, unless it came out of the ark, of course, I wouldn't.'

'The ark's a likely place for it – did you ever see bars held up and the picture of a tiger or something pulled across behind them, so that it looks like it's really prowling?'

'Goodness, did they still play at that in your youth?'

'Shut up.'

'Trick cardboard cut-outs – is that what you are?'

'That's right.'

'Well, I just hope no-one takes away the bars, that's all.'

'Oh, there's no-one will do that.'

'I can sleep safe at night then.'

'You can sleep safe at night.' He grinned.

I gave him the paper and he took it, but he laid it on top of the chest of drawers and set his elbow down on it, as though he was resisting being bullied, but calmly so, because his ability to resist was not in any doubt.

I might have given him the impression of putting two and two together, but I knew nothing of course, and had not guessed much. Only enough to reflect that the main difference between us lay not in our ages, nor in our states of health, nor even in our cultural and political poles, but in the simple fact that he had a cause and I didn't.

While I sat counting the threads in the worn patches of the rugs in the Hungry Cheese and tracing patterns in the hearthstones there, he was defending Wales as though it was about to be over-run.

'Quite a devastating fire last night.'

'Yes.' He sounded more wary of what I might say than of what I might know, and it provoked me to sarcasm.

'Pity the only result will be that the Birmingham owners will make a packet on the insurance.'

'What result would you like to see?' Aled enquired, looking evenly at me. Were I to say I would like to see the arsonists in jail, he would doubtless reply, in a voice as even as his look, that they already were.

100

'Oh I was speaking merely from a nationalist point of view.'

'Then don't – speak from your own.'

'Alright. I've never, personally, quite been able to see the satisfaction in cutting your nose to spite your face – though I've known so many children carry the habit to such outrageous lengths that I'm sure there must be some. . .'

'Those cottages had already been destroyed in all the rebuilding the Brum folk had done,' Aled said, but so indifferently I wondered whether, after all, he had had anything to do with the burning of them. But the next moment he turned on me with a passion I had not seen in him before: 'In any case, I wouldn't have thought you were in much of a position to criticise nationalists for destroying their heritage.'

'Unless you learn to overlook the language I speak, I shall never learn to overlook your youth,' I told him facetiously, and there the conversation seemed to stick. So, to give him an opening to leave, I offered to lend him the paper. 'Lend, mind,' I warned, to make sure, also, that I would see him again.

He borrowed the book of engravings as well.

Afterwards, I went for a walk, turning up the valley, away from the town, but this time keeping to the road, to avoid the Abbey. The miles dropped back and the valley narrowed and the hillsides closed in, and fields of corn took over from animals, blowing between the tree-covered slopes like a ribbon of fouled sand.

There had been no harvesting. The season for it had come and had gone and no doubt, while I had been watching the rain from my room, men had been watching, from the barns, their fields of wheat grow ripe, then over-ripe. In a couple of weeks the strands of golden waves, that must have rippled and shone like silk, had become these acres of sodden, flattened and matted tufts – coarse dark hair that was once dyed blond and has long since needed re-dyeing. The crop was ruined.

There was nothing soothing, nothing soothing at all, about the rhythm of the seasons. There might be ripening and there might be decay, time upon time, flowing across the countryside, but it was a rhythm fractious as the undulations of wind through corn. Time and again the blackening would set in when the ears were still tinged with green, and time and again, mildew took the young grain while it was still soft. And all that could be done was to watch the blundering heavens through the human cycles (equally disorderly) of impatience, tension and despair.

I was half way through. Half the waiting was done, but half the waiting was still to come and I was impatient to get it over with. To learn what had to be learnt, and face what had to be faced after surgery. Then, knowing where I stood, I would be free to be myself again.

It was an illusion, of course. There would always be other, worse things to wait for. The first recurrence. The second recurrence. The third. Then, waiting to lose hope. . .

I was making myself giddy, watching the clouds race under my feet in the mirror-wet road. I might have been some giant treading the cloud-mass, turning the world, and I thought that maybe these few short weeks were the best I would ever have. They were, after all, a reprieve. Nothing could be certain, until the thing in my head was stretched out under a microscope in the pathology labor-atory. For just these few brief weeks, while the consultant was on holiday, I could lose myself in uncertainty. I ought to be able to want to go on and on in uncertainty for ever – go on and on as the road did, winding through all the muddled hills of Wales like a skein of wool that a cat has been let loose with, tangled into a knot such as you could believe the eternity of.

But the road was not going to release me for any sort of eternity. I crossed a bridge and I read 'Cofia Tryweryn' on its parapet, and 'Cofia Abergele' I was urged further on, by the crenellated wall of a tumbledown farm. 'Cofia, cofia' everywhere, exhorting me to remember, remember, when I had come there specifically to blot things out. To forget I had ever existed in any way other than this: to forget there was any other way to exist. All I sought was to be as faceless figuratively as I was literally. And what happened? Just when you thought you were safe, choosing the middle of nowhere to lose your identity in, the struggles inherited from defeated ancestors leapt out at you from country waysides.

It was a vandalised landscape: yet it wasn't mine as much as Aled's. Aled would not have needed the painted words to be reminded of Tryweryn and of Abergele. The ground itself would hint to him of the blowing up of reservoirs and deaths at the investitures of princes. Where I saw slanting woods he would see the tunnels that undermined them, pitting them like the pores in a sponge, and the men who had been set to dig there, to whom the planning of explosions must have come as second nature.

It would be nothing to Aled, all this rotting corn: one lost harvest was hardly here or there in a lost country.

It would be a long while yet before it would give him my sense of waste, of wasted time. Too long. For by the time you realise youth is the one and only thing no-one can ever take away from you, it has vanished of its own accord.

When I got to the Hungry Cheese that evening, Aled was sitting where I always sat.

He looked rather tentative. (True, I had felt a twinge of territorial right.)

He also looked uncomfortable, bolt upright, with his hands clasped over my paper on awkwardly jutting knees.

'H'm. If you're aiming at backache and stiff knees I'd say you were showing tolerable promise.'

As he was obviously not going to move, I sat beside him, but I wouldn't meet his eyes.

'Showing tolerable promise! I can see you writing that on school reports – being careful to qualify any approval.'

'Any approval of you is certainly qualified.' I had meant to speak with calm irony, but it came out cattily, for a lump had come into my throat. Careful was I? Well, I hadn't been careful enough not to mention I'd been a teacher, had I? Even though I knew that anything you told anyone was bound to rebound on you.

He might not have meant to be cruel. But I had enjoyed teaching.

With the lightning agility with which he had stooped for a stone at the caravans, Aled leapt up and stood in front of me, frowning. 'You sit there' – he indicated his seat – 'and I'll get you a drink.'

I suppose, seeing me upset, he thought it was because he had taken my seat.

I had enjoyed teaching.

And I had never written 'showing tolerable promise' on anyone's report – it was hardly English.

'You're the only woman I know who drinks whisky neat.' A loner like Aled, generalising on women's tastes! But he mustn't have known what to say, returning with the drinks and finding I hadn't moved up.

'How the hell do you manage to fold into this blasted bench anyway?' He tried to imitate the way I sat, but he was too long and seemed to bend in the wrong places and I laughed.

'It's no good – you just haven't got the required strict Puritanical bearing.'

He glanced involuntarily at the paper, and lifted it to spread it. I looked at it too, at the stumbling figures between the police, bowed like murderers: the posture of humiliation, or simply a turning aside to avoid recognition.

Aled's face was hard and set. He might similarly have flinched from cameras at his own arrest. Or he might not. Looking at him drew his eyes to mine; instantly, we both looked away.

'I would feel differently, Aled, if they had needed somewhere to live.'

'Would you?' Cold, sarcastic, nearly sneering.

'If they had nowhere to go,' I pleaded.

'Because you have nowhere to go.'

'No. Not because of that.'

And yet leaving hospital was an appalling prospect I did not care to contemplate.

How had he guessed I had given up my flat?

'Anyway, squatting's not the issue. They're being "taken in for questioning" – must be in connection with something else.'

'Must it?' This time he was openly sneering.

'Well you can't be arrested for squatting, can you?'

'Exactly.'

'You mean the "wanted for questioning" bit is just a pretext for dragging them out?' I challenged incredulously.

He said nothing.

'Oh Aled!'

Then I asked: 'Do you know them?'

'Who?'

'The – people being questioned.'

'As well as I know the people doing the questioning.'

Oh dear.

He gave me back the paper. 'Maybe,' he said, 'they won't come up with the right questions. After all, Peredur didn't.'

Old whatsisname again: but this time he struck a chord.

'Failing to ask the right question might bring havoc,' I said tartly, 'but who's to say learning the answer wouldn't be as bad, or worse?'

The surprise on his face gave me a moment's satisfaction (though I wasn't sure whether it was because I knew the story or because I questioned its assumptions).

I thought it best not to mention that in my version it hadn't been whatsisname who had failed to ask the question that would have prevented the devastation of the land, but Percival. No doubt the Mabinogion and T.S. Eliot met, somewhere out there in the waste land: no culture, it seems, can do without its chaos.

'Ah, but by the time you've found the right question to ask, you've already got an inkling as to the answer,' Aled insisted.

'All the more reason to evade the right question.'

'How can you evade it without knowing what it is?'

I was not going on with this nonsense: he, I supposed, was off on some obscure political tack, while I was talking about what I should, or should not, have said to my prospective surgeon. And no abstractions can cope for long with that breadth of topic.

'If you already know the answer to a question there's precious little point in asking it,' I announced, with finality.

Aled had the grace to behave as though he had been defeated.

He got up to poke the fire. 'You're not drying off much by this.' There was just one little flame dancing bravely along an immature log, like a child nervously shifting along an overhanging limb.

I didn't care how ineffectual it was. It was a friendly little thing; if wayward.

'Potentially destructive,' warned Aled, as if correcting my school report.

I glanced down at the paper, lying now in my lap. The houses behind the people being taken away by the police would no doubt feature on the front page of the next edition too. But this time, only the fire-brigade would be in the foreground.

Ceri's mates arrived.

I moved my feet to let Aled pass, but he did not budge, nor did he show any awareness of the punks' entry, or of my deference.

That first evening we sat together, they showed how conscious they were of us – casting the odd quick glance at Aled, as if to check he was alive without wanting to seem obsessive (like young mothers), and more lingering glances at me, intrigued, appraising, mistrusting. And that evening, Ceri never came.

But on later nights he did, and after a long cool stare at the two of us, he ignored us completely. The others imitated him (for the weak Ceri was striking, suddenly, some kind of devil-may-care lead), and Aled was ignored altogether. But I was not. Aled had only to get up to go to the bar, or go to the toilet, and they smirked openly at me, or smacked their mouths in cheeky, pouting kisses, or made more obscene sexual advances. I could only look away in disdain, feeling a mixture of bitter self-consciousness and depression, and half hoping Aled would surprise them at it, but they were always too quick for that. Ceri took no part in all this tormenting; but Douglas did.

I suppose time hung heavily on all of us, oppressive as the September skies, with their weight of rainclouds, hardly moving. But it seemed aeons since Ceri had played pool with me, or since they had all been content to have me serve as umpire in their dart games.

The night I felt most goaded of all, was when they were mercilessly enacting the gruesome kind of deformities they felt they could expect from nuclear war.

Never, never, never, must they so much as suspect I was growing a tumour in me.

I could see them so vividly, affecting to surreptitiously wipe their glasses in case I had drunk from them, shrinking back from me in melodramatic horror, as from a leper. All genuinely comical.

106

And I cursed, again, my foolishness in telling the things I had told to Aled.

And, looking at his thin form and faded arms, and the flecks of his freckles, covering his face like a sprinkling of autumn leaves falling on a new corpse in the forest, I cursed my distrust of him too.

CHAPTER EIGHT

The heat was persisting – depressingly, week after week, the stifling, muggy heat. Heat bound the country like a heavy cloud of atmospheric pollution: rain fell into it and evaporated, leaving the air more muggy still, and the sun that tried to burn through was so fuzzy it did not even lift the greyness from off the surface of things.

I kept thinking how different things would be if the weather cleared. If the weather would only clear. . . If it cleared, I could get my bearings, take stock, get organised.

But the heat persisted and persisted and I was limp and feeble, capable of doing nothing but waiting for it to clear. Hoping it would clear while there was still time. Huddled over the little fires that Thomas built; taking comfort from them, though in the end all they did was make the heat worse.

I took to walking in the woods on the hillsides where the valley narrowed, to make the old twigs there scrunch and crackle under my feet like kindling, causing consternation to the birds and the squirrels, making believe that I had the power to cause crises yet. . .

'Talking of crises. . .' interrupted Aled when I told him, and stopped.

I waited.

It was lunch-time. Aled had begun coming to the Hungry Cheese for lunch.

'Ceri Griff's in bother.'

'Oh? What now?'

'He's just driven down Ystrad Cwmhir in zig-zags, clocking up shoppers and dogs and making cars crash and ending up among the vegetables he demolished outside Simkins.'

All things considered, that little market town must feature in the *Western Mail* more often than the size of its population warranted.

'Anyone hurt?'

'Bruising seemed the general effect.'

'Driven?'

'Nicked a bike. Having been disqualified. And while on probation.'

Thomas had not told me about the probation.

'Oh God.'

'Oh God's about right.'

'Poor Ceri.'

'Helpful, that.'

'Poor Ceri all the same.'

'Why? I wouldn't have thought you'd have much time for juvenile delinquency!'

'Time? How do you know what I have time for and what I haven't?' I told him about standing in a queue for plums, just after the hospital, with all the time in the world and yet without a moment to lose (and, incidentally, without much desire for plums), and being overtaken by a sudden, intolerable anger. There I was, feebly paying homage to little social niceties, when I'd just been given a tumour. So I strode up to the counter and pushed in, rudely as I could, and browbeat the girl into serving me.

'And she did?'

'Yes. Yes, she did. People sometimes give you what you want in order to get rid of you.'

'Not if you're Ceri Griff they don't. People hang on to Ceri Griff and send for the police.'

'Well I hope he got more of a kick out of his defiance than I got out of mine.'

'He'll get a kick *for* it the moment I catch up with him.' But Aled looked dejected rather than angry, stirring with his toe the accumulation of fine log-ash that had spilled out onto the flagstones, and tracing primitive swirls in it until I wanted him to stop making any more patterns I couldn't fathom the meaning of.

'Surely it's not that serious – surely the worst he'll get will be longer probation?' Aled did not answer. 'I can't see why you're so surprised Ceri should freak out.'

109

Aled mussed up the swirls impatiently with his foot.

'If one of your pupils had done what Ceri Griff did, you wouldn't have hoped he'd "got a kick out of it" would you?'

I felt rather unable to explain I'd only recently discovered what it was like when you couldn't keep up with your friends.

'If it had been one of your pupils,' Aled persisted, 'wouldn't you have blamed his parents or something?'

I said nothing.

'Wouldn't you? Say.'

I was too tired to keep up the resistance of silence. So I said: 'I suspect I might have been more inclined to have blamed someone like you.'

It startled him.

'Well, you ask and you ask, and you ought to have learnt from the plums that I can't be tactful any more.'

This time, we both let the silence be. There was only the tiny crunching of ash that Aled turned and turned under his foot. Scraping it together into a heap, patting it flat, flatter, flatter, until it spread apart; scraping it together again. He might have been trying to knead it into a cement, but the ash refused to adhere.

The long evenings of doing it had burned, along the side of his shoe, a dark stain.

'Freaking out and breaking the law has nothing to do with breaking it for a purpose,' he said at last.

'It's all breaking the law.'

'So you think it's worse to break laws for good reasons than it is to go berserk and break them for the sheer hell of it?'

'Oh Aled, I don't know.'

'You don't know?'

'I only know that Ceri's not a frightening person, and you are.'

'Frightening?'

'Yes. Cold-blooded murder is frightening in a way that hot-blooded murder isn't.'

I expected him to baulk at the gratuitous talk of murder, but he didn't.

'Even if the victim of a hot-blooded murder is a child, and the victim of a cold-blooded one is someone like Hitler?'

'Yes.'

'Good God, Ann – are you some kind of fascist or what? Freaking out is quite safe, is it, because it burns itself out – but anything organised is to be feared and stamped out?'

I told him he was the fascist, imposing his ideas of right and wrong on others quite regardless that people on the whole didn't agree with them.

'On the whole?' he interrupted. 'What the fuck is "on the whole"? Boundaries are wherever you choose to draw them.'

But I clung tenaciously to my point. 'Ceri can break the law in ways you approve of, can't he, but just let him watch out if he breaks it in ways you frown upon, down Ystrad Cwmhir. Hasn't it got shades of knee-capping, this "kick" you are about to administer?'

But it wasn't the way I should have challenged him; I should have challenged him without sarcasm, as he had challenged me: openly, about what it was they dragged to and fro along the fire-escapes at night, about his involvement in arson. I ought to have faced him squarely, but I couldn't. I couldn't. I had had my fill of facing things. I just didn't want to know anything, any more.

Abruptly, Aled cooled off. 'I'm annoyed because he's wrecking himself, that's all. I'm not going to touch him, for Christ's sake. You know that.'

But I can't really have known it in the way he supposed, for when Thomas marched over to us one evening just outside the hotel, and rounded on Aled for putting Ceri Griff through one of his windows, I instantly assumed Aled had been punishing Ceri for his escapade.

Aled stood embarrassed, refusing to look at Thomas, muttering that the window would be replaced of course.

'What happened?' I asked, but they ignored me, Thomas so angry that my presence didn't seem to have registered, and Aled mortified at Thomas confronting him in front of me.

'Replaced when?' Thomas insisted.

'Just as soon as is humanly possible.' Aled's uncannily pink lips were drawn in a thin, bitter line. He was staring back, now, into

111

Thomas's grotesquely bulging eyeballs. 'It only happened last night.'

'You'd hardly miss a window or two in this heat,' I said.

Thomas noticed me then, and seemed about to test my hypothesis by putting me through a second of his windows. I stepped back smartly, then stood stunned by the viciousness with which he spat out: '*You* can just keep your mouth shut. If it hadn't been for you, none of this would have happened.'

'*Cau dy geg,*' cut in Aled, preventing me speaking, but I was too taken aback at the idea that I had somehow laid a curse upon the hotel, to say anything anyway. Aled talked rapidly for a while, and Thomas became calm, but inward and unrelenting.

'What did you mean?' I asked, when Aled let him alone, but Thomas was ignoring me again.

'What did you mean?' I demanded. 'You accused me of causing whatever's happened. You owe me an explanation. At the very least!' I was back among the furniture of my school office.

There was no response. 'Alright.' I turned to Aled: 'What did happen?'

He, at least, met my eyes, but one eyebrow lifted in comic, bemused refusal.

'I want to know what you meant by saying it was my fault,' I persisted grimly to Thomas.

Thomas gave in. 'All it was about. . .' he began as though I was the one making all the fuss, but Aled's face had turned, and Thomas paused, obviously disconcerted by the other's fiery eyes. Then, looking to heaven, with an air of being exasperated beyond endurance by the pair of us, he concluded cursorily: 'Ceri Griff was being rude about you and Aled Owen put him through a window – that's all.' Washing his hands of the whole affair, he went back into his hotel.

I had only to look at Aled to know it was true, and I had only to look at Aled to smother all the questions and indignation and fantastic notions confusedly bubbling in my head. His controlled fury had gone. He stood beside me like some stubborn child, the stubborn child I had faced a hundred times across my desk – exposed, defeated, humiliated, yet hopelessly defiant still, eyes

112

fixed on the blank wall behind me, patient of my amusement or my anger, indifferent to both. But with this particular child, all the paraphernalia of the office fell away from around me.

I walked away from him, aware, faintly, of the sound of running water somewhere ahead; drawn to it, rather like a thirsty animal, or like the sick – or like the dying, not able to drink, but needing the presence of water close at hand.

I stood there for some time, watching the stream swill between the walls of houses and then disappear into a pipe under the road.

When I looked round, I saw Aled sitting on the wall of the little bridge where the stream emerged, the other side of the road. He was watching me.

I crossed over. 'Do you know what?' I said as though it was a matter for annoyance. 'There are bloody fish presuming to live in this stream. You stop for a minute and you look at the filthy, greasy water and you see all the muck it's carrying down in it, and you think what a vile place it is you're in. And then, blow me, if there isn't a silvery flash under the slime, and some silly fish goes and does a somersault or something, and you have to revise your view of things. It's like finding you in the world.'

Aled's face didn't alter, nor did he move, but there was awkwardness in his limbs, as though they had gone stiff. So I went on, in the same matter-of-fact tone: 'Bring that book of engravings back, would you please, Aled. I want to get it back to the library before I forget about it and end up with a fine I cannot afford.'

It was always best to be brutal and dismissive, but when I went up to my room, I felt like a different person going in through the door. Whatever it was that Ceri had said about me, whatever the truth of Aled's reaction, and however warped and tangled were the emotions between the two of them, and between each of them and me, I had aroused, pathetic as I was, some kind of loyalty in a human being.

I looked out beyond the uneven and discoloured wood of the fire-escapes, and beyond the crumbling brick chimneys to the clouds, without begrudging them the freedom of their mindless, endless passing. The indifference of the world had, for one violent instant, been stopped.

But I pictured beside me Aled's face, the eyebrows raised in mild sarcasm, reminding me that violence was violence was violence. And I imagined the tired, soft voice asking what attitude I used to take when one child put another through a classroom window.

I couldn't, actually, remember it ever happening, but I suppose if it had, I would fairly have wiped the floor with the culprit. And had the misguided youngster inadvertently revealed he had been acting on my behalf I would doubtless have expressed particular disgust that he should consider I needed that kind of defence.

Oh dear, we do grow pitiful.

But I let the feeling of warmth and of gratitude come, and I did welcome it. Despite the unforgettable grey eyes, no longer sarcastic, bidding me repay him then, by coming clean about where my own loyalties lay – daring me to take my suspicions to the police.

The sun came out briefly, glinting on broken glass that lay in the yard.

And yes, above it the jagged edges of plate glass framing a black hole.

Oh my God.

Ceri must be hurt. I hadn't thought, but Ceri must be hurt.

Ceri, bursting through that, and the thousand jewels and daggers of glass flying like the shapes in the painting in the Hungry Cheese, but more weird, more angular, more deadly. Black against the spraying blood.

Whatever could he have said, to make Aled do that?

I drew the curtains and sat on the bed, doubling up, frightened. Frightened for Ceri, frightened of what Aled had done, frightened of Aled. Frightened of the things that were not explained, and of the ugly hole, and of what would happen next.

But fears shift easily, and we are fickle things, and everyone's immersed in their own fate.

How was it that I had heard nothing, when a lump of solid flesh had mashed sheet glass, in the next wing?

I went back to the window, to check just how close the broken pane was.

I had suspected for some time that I was going deaf on the side where the tumour was.

114

So close. How was it I had not heard Aled put Ceri through that window in the night?

It was beginning to be dusk, and the bats were flittering blindly around the eaves, swooping and dodging and darting, never free, never sure. I thought how full of obstacles the world must seem, when you had to rely for knowledge of it on the reverberations of your own cries. And yet how skilled you became, even then, in avoiding things. . .

I remembered the cries – high, urgent, persistent screams, that only a child could hear without shuddering.

Now, the little deformed animals flitted around me in complete silence.

It was the normal deafness of age, the normal deafness of age.

But how could it have been that I had not heard Aled put Ceri through that window?. . .

The next morning, and for two days after that, I read all the papers that the library took. There was no mention of Ceri. But neither did he reappear in the Hungry Cheese, nor in the junk-room, nor with the machines; and the roof-space where I had first disturbed him dossing down had been blocked off. Occasionally I fancied I caught him skulking round a corner, but it would turn out to be a cat, or something blowing in the draught from the gas-fire shafts, or a shadow, or an eyelash, or just nothing.

I watched the malevolent way Thomas screwed the teatowel round glass after glass, and then set each down as menacingly as if it were a weapon, and I dared ask him nothing.

But I listened. I listened to the gang while they ragged one another and bickered, and I strained to listen to their subdued conferring, but the familiar, unintelligible words never seemed to contain the syllables of 'Ceri Griff'. So I watched their features and their gestures, in case an allusion should be hidden there, and I noticed how their hands perpetually fluttered, like bats, while mine lay locked around my whisky: and I saw, too, how unmarked their faces were in the dim light of the place, with never any sign of regret, or concern, or thought, for anyone who was not there.

It was as though Ceri had never existed.

115

They might have lost their scapegoat, but Aled was taking over as peacemaker among them. They basked somehow in the glow of reconciliation with him, and he seemed amused at the conflicts between their striving to please, and their striving for attention. But in the intervals when he sat beside me, the bitterness on the rugged face, and the unyielding crossed arms, were as forbidding as the contortions of Thomas's towel, twisting in the fragile glass.

Eventually, I forced myself to ring the local hospital, but they sounded wary of me and had no casualty department anyway. So I rang the hospitals at Newtown and at Aberystwyth, and they were businesslike in their certainty that no-one of the name I mentioned was on their books.

Dissatisfied, I sent 'get well' cards to them all, but they all came back. Thomas was very suspicious that, at this stage, I should suddenly begin receiving mail.

I felt entangled in some con-game that reminded me of my first days in the place, when everything seemed to be conspiring to rid me of the illusion that I was real. Only now it was Ceri who was being wiped out.

Finally, I just would not, childishly would not, have it.

'Aled, where is Ceri?'

'Ceri Griff is avoiding us.' Prompt, and very formal. Aled had patently seen the question coming for days.

'Avoiding us?'

'Avoiding us.'

'Us?' I hadn't put Ceri through anything.

'Us.'

'Us?' Inelegantly I threw out a hand to embrace the whole room.

'The two of us.'

'Us two?'

'He thinks we're having an affair.'

'He thinks what?'

I could do nothing but stare; Aled's eyes closed. How dare they? How dare they. . . mock me. . . between them? How could they – the pair of them?

Aled, setting me up for Ceri to knock.

116

(Me setting Aled up for Ceri to knock?)

Ceri was the one who had been knocked. . .

'Was that what putting him through the window was all about?'

The eyes opened, steel-grey and fierce, fixed on mine. 'No.' They closed again.

But how could I believe that? How could I ever believe that? What else could it have been?

So it hadn't been loyalty at all: Aled had been defending himself from the insulting accusation of a liaison with me. Defending his own dignity.

Well, I had no call to feel cheated – it was my own stupid fancies that had imputed loyalty to Aled. And it was no use feeling betrayed into revealing my feelings – in any case, I had only called the fellow a fish.

A fish was what he was, too, a cold, cold fish.

'There's a cruel streak in you, Aled, isn't there?'

I got no reaction.

His closed eyelids were so delicate you could see the interlacings of the blood-vessels there. Vulnerable hollows, exposed when he was least aware. With the shaggy eyebrows standing guard above them, like a snow-laden hedge sheltering blue and rose-pink trellised tendrils.

Ceri must hate him now.

And Aled must have been quite wrong, thinking that Ceri had been ashamed towards me. Ceri had not been shunning me out of shame.

To Ceri, we were just so much filth.

The face of a fatherless boy I had once taught came back to me – a nondescript lad, Huw something or other, who took off to some seventh heaven when his sixth-form hero picked him up for a lark. And the seventh heaven lasted too, lasted longer than one would have thought possible – lasted, in fact, until the day the child surprised the older boy with his mother. You don't forget the way a child sits in class after that.

'Well, Ceri must be disabused of the absurd notion, that's all.'

Aled laughed bitterly, but stopped short, as though weary suddenly of the false sound.

117

He was finding, for the first time perhaps, that there is nothing so debilitating as being despised.

'It's none of his business.'

Aled, of course, would meet contempt with contempt.

It went harder on him than it did on me, for Ceri had worshipped him.

'No, but you can understand his horror once the idea got fixed in his head, can't you? And it's only natural he should react with disgust, isn't it? I mean, just look at me!'

I opened the fists curled in my lap, making the skin wrinkle and the middle joints buckle, ugly as knees, yellowish. Fists that had knocked Ceri for six.

But Aled did not look at them. He looked instead as though, between me and Ceri, there really was more to cope with than he had bargained for.

It seemed that things were going to be left up to me.

When I pondered on the practicalities of explaining to Ceri that I had not seduced Aled, however, there did seem difficulties. Ceri had, for a start, disappeared. And even if he hadn't, the whole idea of any such encounter went utterly against the grain. I didn't feel at all like the humiliation of it. Besides, it was ludicrous to suppose I could even deal reasonably with his adolescent fantasies, never mind conquer them. I could imagine Ceri staring back stupidly, or superciliously lifting that weak chin of his and looking down that small tilted nose with immense scorn, as if to say – 'whatever makes you think I'd even dream that anyone like you could seduce someone like Aled?'

Oh, botheration.

I began with the other large hotel in town, modern, with young, listless staff and hot, bad-tempered patrons. It was busy enough for no-one to pay me any attention as I strode down the foyer and through the fire-doors into the inner precinct of the corridors. (Doubtless they were used to people coming in off the street to use the toilets with just the same too-purposeful stride.) But unless he was hiding in the Gents, or in one of the bedrooms, Ceri was not there.

I quailed at the gates of the two small hotels: they looked far too

118

like guest-houses for anything approaching a discreet search. Also, though they might well sport a pool table, machines, I felt, would be beyond the pale.

I did the round of the pubs, and I found him in the end, in the Golden Goose.

I peered into the corner of gloom where the noise was coming from – the dead ring of money in the slot, the ping, the thump, the snap, the whirr; and there was Ceri's face, abruptly lit by the flashing lights playing round the strips of fruit. He hardly waited to see what came up before he was pressing money into the slot again.

The vacant, broken chairs between us seemed to leer, like so many inebriated customers competing in a game of statues, frozen in grotesque attitudes when the music stopped.

And high on the dingy walls, rows of old cracked mirrors hung, with the expressionless faces of seamen advertising cigarettes in a parody of ancestral portraits.

In one of the mirrors I caught a reflected movement.

There was a man just behind me, an old man, fussing like a vole, his mittened fingers tweaking at the folds of his torn mac. Another – two, three more: a whole row of them; old men, each alone, arrayed along the wall like a jury – as if they were adjudicating the chairs' bizarre dance.

There seemed to be no-one behind the bar.

I sat down.

The row of cloth caps and pints were like bread and water set before a line of prisoners.

Ceri was concentrating on the mechanically swirling pieces of fruit as intently as if he were still manoeuvring space machines.

There was a tinkling of coins. Without breaking the rhythm of his game, Ceri scooped them up.

He won again, and again.

Out of the blue I heard chuckling. A tall old man who had been sitting stiffly upright as if in rigor mortis, had come to life: mischievous eyes crinkled, and winked at a neighbour. It was like a signal. One by one they perked up and grew alert. Ceri's improbable gains were breaking through their vegetating. They were willing him to win, as though his change of luck affected them too – as though it avenged the ill-fate of them all.

Mindlessly, obsessively, Ceri inserted coin after coin. And still he won.

There was no approaching him on that high.

The roguish glee of the old men died away; apathetically they turned back to their solitary pints, the lot they had had to settle for. Perhaps they had simply been unsettled by the variation in the noises of the game, before growing accustomed to it.

The sniffling of the man in mittens, however, was becoming the sniffling of discontent. His eyes ran too: it was as if he was wax melting in the heat of his uneasiness.

Still the coins trickled down.

Heads began to strain towards the bar, showing concern, then frustration, at the absence of the landlord. They frowned at one another; turned back urgently to the bar. To me, indignantly.

The man in mittens must have mistaken me for the barmaid. He beckoned, and jabbed towards the machine that had gone bananas and ought to be put a stop to.

When I ignored him, he struggled to get to his feet, but he began to gasp, like a bird whose neck is only half wrung, and clutch at the table. His nails squealed the length of its plastic surface as he fell back, his eyes maligning me.

Let Ceri be damned, playing fast and loose with the fickleness of these old men, and setting them like dogs at me. Let him be damned, him and all the talent he was debasing on a fruit machine. Having the audacity to spurn me for cheapening myself, cheapening Aled, and then prostituting himself here! Let him go to hell!

CHAPTER NINE

All the hundred shades of green there had been in the valley, had gone. It was as if the whisky had spilled from my glass in the Hungry Cheese and steeped the whole land.

The summer was done.

But it was from the soil, that gold – it had been oozing out of the soil ever since I had come there – seeping up into the stalks of the young corn and into the ears of wheat and barley, and out through the trembling whiskers on their tips.

From there, as the corn faded and then darkened, the gold had sprayed upwards, catching the lowest leaves on the trees and in the hedgerows, turning them pale. And once it had caught it spread, moving upwards still, more confidently; flaming up into the tops of the trees just as the lower leaves dropped out of its reach, tarnishing and withering, and falling onto the rotting corn. And from the valley floor, the gold swung up through the plantations of larch covering the hillsides, sliding like sunshine that pours from a leaden sky and floods across the landscape, immersing even the last few needles on the topmost fronds on the skyline. We walked down in the shadow one evening, Aled and I, and watched them high above us, fluttering and straining like shining prayer-flags, and as we watched, the gold seemed to surge on up again, breaking out among the clouds and fanning across the sky like a great stain stealing over the earth. But the quality of it was changed: this wasn't the rich gold that had crept from the ground into the seeds of corn, but a weak diluted gold turning more yellow as the sun set – turning into the hue that jaundice casts upon the skin. And in the end, as night fell, it didn't seem to be a glorious ripeness that had burst forth at all, but an infection, that had got out of control and swept across the world, and was leaving the land barren as it passed away.

I told Aled it was as though his head had been buried and its pallor had flushed up from the soil and taken over the country.

It was a tactless thing to say. Aled looked away into the bruised sky, frowning, and I smarted under it with him.

I had only said it to show him that, in spite of everything, I wasn't totally immune to the heritage that was lost to me.

But to substitute him for Bendigeidfran or for Arthur like that had been horribly unkind.

No doubt he was left thinking it had been easy enough for men who had marched down these valleys at the head of armies, to leave promises of national resurgence, but it was quite a different tale for their descendants, who found themselves lurking around caravans concealed behind the ruins of abbeys, and mustering their supporters in secret (well, relative secret) along roughly-made fire-escapes around the back yards of unfrequented hotels.

'One of them old tombs, supposed to be, round here. Game to look for it?'

Already dusk, and barbed wire, and Aled not helping me over.

Trailing into the bracken after his long, stooped spine that might have borne, lodged within it, a bullet too deeply embedded to be removed, the lead of which was drawing his flesh and gradually poisoning his whole system (if such a thing were possible).

Not a man of any renown. Not even a strong man. But in nettles and ragwort and hawthorn and rowan, he found the tomb. And then, what did the strong ever have over the weak, bar a lack of imagination and the incapacity to doubt themselves?

It was a dolmen merely: three standing stones and a collapsed capstone: the smallest standing stone at a rakish angle. If there had ever been any mound it had worn, or been ploughed, away.

All we knew of people, in the end, was the custom of their death. And of us, no-one would even know that (unless they were to guess from the absence of evidence).

'I wonder if these are anything,' Aled called, and I went over to look.

'Weathering.'

'Scrawls like that?'

'Weathering. Or a drawing of the sun or moon or waves or wind. All weather.'

'Jesus, Ann.'

'Oh for heaven's sake Aled! What do I know about you – never mind about people who make Arthur look recent?'

'But they stood here, Ann, straining away, levering up this twenty-ton roof. . .'

'And not quite managing it. . .'

'And all for what?'

'Oh, some glorious dream or other, no doubt – I don't suppose we've changed as much as that.'

'What's wrong with dreams?'

'Huh!'

'Go on – what's wrong with them?'

'Well, how do you feel when you look back on the kind of things you used to dream of?'

'Um – how do you feel?'

'Pretty contemptuous.'

'Oh.'

'But defensive, too, about the way I was then. That's what makes it painful, isn't it?'

'Is it?' He was leaning casually against the vast stone that had intrigued him, his feet crossed, rocking on his ankles; more interested now in the unripe sloe he was dissecting.

'What was it you dreamt of doing with your life, Aled, when you were younger?'

'What I dream of doing now, I guess.'

'Oh. I wonder if that could be what's frightening about you?'

'What's frightening about opening a Welsh bookshop?' He flung his fistful of sloes far over my head.

I looked at him, but he wasn't teasing, or confiding in me – he was merely impatient with me.

Opening a bookshop was what he would do when the economy revived, or when his circumstances changed, or after the re-volution. While we all waited, I made my gesture of resistance in one way, and Ceri in another: only Aled was resisting calmly and sensibly and purposefully.

Opening a bookshop. I hadn't expected anything like that.

Would he ever really open a bookshop?

There were clusters of berries already on the rowan beside us.

'Things can be dreams for too long, Aled,' I said, with the gloom of hindsight on a youth spent in the Sixties, when we were so often told we'd never had it so good, we'd thought the world a place we could always fall back on.

But Aled, still young in the Eighties, thought I meant Welsh would be dead if he waited much longer.

'Killing a language is like killing an octopus, you know. Not simple, like killing a man.'

He was sprawled now against the massive slab – his outflung arms grasping its sides as though he steeled himself for the sacrifice, or challenged the gods. I turned away, hating all that smooth stone slabs have ever meant to things of flesh.

'And this bookshop would activate one tiny muscle in one arm of the octopus.' I sounded resentful of my own role of malfunctioning cell.

'What else can you do?'

You tell me, I thought, uncertain, suddenly, of all my suspicions; puzzled that he should sound depressed and not sarcastic.

'What else, indeed!'

'Disparaging bitch of a schoolmistress!'

Yes. But reducing him to despair was the only way I knew of creating closeness between us.

'I didn't mean... you know when I said don't dream too long... I didn't mean what you thought I meant.'

'Come on, anyway – it's dark and I'm not really any more fascinated by the stone age than you are.'

We walked in single file back through the cornfields, skirting the crops as though under the illusion they might yet be harvested.

'When I visit your bookshop, I'll confront everything you want the world to learn, and all I'll see will be my own ignorance.'

'Ah well, you'll be able to look at the pictures.'

When he didn't help now, over the fences, it wasn't out of pique – it was just that he wasn't going to defer to me. Which is all very well if you haven't gone in search of the stone age in a pleated skirt and shoes which not the thickest of your ancestors would have called flat (if they had such a word).

We had to hurry along the road, to get to the Hungry Cheese in time.

'You think I know nothing about what it's like to face losing the way you've seen the world, and felt and thought about it, don't you? But it isn't only when your language is under threat that you can lose all those things, you know.'

'Don't keep slowing down. It isn't that. It's the tragedy of nobody being able to read great books – marvellous books by people who have thought deeply and created imaginatively – books that have made a lot of us what we are – and only the death of a language does that.'

'Yes, I can understand that. . .'

'Can you?'

'But what do you think it's like spending your whole life in your own country without being able to speak its language?'

'Alright I imagine; otherwise you'd do something about learning it.'

'I did. You do. And what you find is that, far from helping, you lot close ranks on us. Feeling protective is all very well, but it can lead to a kind of smugness which is very exclusive, you know.'

'Don't push it, Ann, or you'll make me think you have a vested interest in wiping Welsh out.'

'It's you that's pushing it.'

And, I thought, rather savagely, what's more, you are probably talking over a background of shrill wailing by these blessed bats, twitching and fooling hysterically around us.

But when we reached the Hungry Cheese we slunk underground with all the relief that primitive man must have felt, ducking to the hearth-fire of his smoke-filled cave. And I wished I had asked Aled what books he meant, instead of getting riled.

But perhaps they would explain less than he thought they did, about people like him. Nothing blotted out the past so absolutely as a blank present, and that, after all, was our point of contact. When there was no work, and you were left to wait your life out, it stopped mattering after a while why Llywelyn died, or what

125

Peredur was committed to, or did, or what question he failed to ask.

'Why don't you want to know anything?' Aled asked, so sadly I smiled in surprise at the thought that perhaps he had wanted to tell me what books he had been talking about.

'I've just lost my nerve for finding things out – that's all,' I apologised.

'Don't you ever wonder what caused it?'

For some reason tears sprang to my eyes as I realised what he was talking about.

'Well. . . as a matter of fact. . . I did ask that, but. . . um. . . it turned out not to be the right question.'

'What did they say?'

'Oh they said. . . um. . .' Stupidly, my voice had got so unsteady I had to pretend, for a moment, not to remember. 'Oh yes – they said it could happen to anyone.'

'Sounds more like the wrong answer than the wrong question.'

I shrugged. 'All I would have discovered anyway was something to blame myself for.'

'That's just plain silly – you'd have discovered a way of preventing another. Some means of control.'

I looked over at the youths picking quarrels like hens in a farmyard, evoking curiosity and boredom both; at Thomas swilling at his sink, dulled or preoccupied; at the red and black shapes prancing in mockery on the broken wall; at the logs' trickles of smouldering starlight. The notion of any means of control was laughable.

'Though I guess, at the moment, you're more bothered about getting rid of the one you've got.'

'I guess,' I agreed dryly, wanting not to speak of it.

'It's the day-to-day resistance that's important isn't it?'

'I don't know – day-to-day survival is fast losing its attractiveness.'

'No – you're a survivor Ann. In your own way. We both are. It's Ceri Griff who isn't.'

'Mm. I can certainly see him coming to a sticky end.' I hadn't said anything to Aled about following him to the Golden Goose, but I was tense with the suspicion that Aled mentioned him to watch my reaction. 'But you just wait. We'll plough on doggedly to the bitter end and he'll kill himself spectacularly. That way he'll outlast us both.'

'Spectacularly?' Aled folded his arms to indulge my fantasising: the freckles on them had smudged.

'Well. . . riding a stolen motorbike across a row of terraced roofs or something – some feat that will become legendary despite its utter purposelessness. In fact we are given to gasping at such idiocy. There doesn't have to be any golden fleece to secure – all you have to do is sail around the world standing on your head, or climb Everest on one leg. Quite the in thing as the country heads for ruin.'

Aled paid the irony no heed, and it struck me that while we might both lurk underground, there was nothing to say that the probing spotlight turning in the swing of the planet would not pick him up for an instant, the way it had caught a thousand others like him.

'Ceri Griff is not that good a driver, you know.'

'Exactly – he'll probably kill himself.'

But Aled can't have thought I was getting the point, for the next day he came in awkwardly half-concealing something he dropped into my lap.

It was a copy of Breughel's painting of The Fall of Icarus that looked as though it had been torn out of a calendar.

'Is this a preview of the pictures you will be stocking for the illiterate?' Seeing him blink slowly with enforced tolerance, I added severely: 'An old calendar I hope.'

Patiently, he waited for a more genuine reaction.

I had none.

He stretched across to point to the tiny legs of Icarus, hardly noticeable in the sea as the boy drowned.

'Ceri Griff.'

I suppose it was to show me that his heroics would go un-noticed, that life would go on uninterrupted, with everyone absorbed in what they were doing.

'But his attempt at flying is legendary! And Breughel's not

denying that is he? Isn't he seeing tragedy in the lack of concern of the world, which is making no attempt to save him?'

'No, there's no tragedy.'

'I suppose for you it's only national aspiration that matters.'

'What's so great about aspiring at all? Anyway, Ceri Griff doesn't aspire – he takes risks out of sheer boredom. Probably Icarus was the same.'

'Boredom's probably been behind a lot of achievement. In any case I wouldn't have thought you were in much of a position to preach about Ceri's boredom.' Neither was I, of course, but that was beside the point.

It was a superficial enough disagreement: Aled recognised, as bitterly as I did, Breughel's truth that the world was given to turning aside from human mischance.

'And there's you.' I nodded at the ploughman in the fore-ground, who had his eyes fixed on the ground even that late in the day, whose body was weary but whose furrow was straight: who was staying on, to get to the end of the field before nightfall: who had no patience with the boy who had flown too close to the sun.

He was quick to return the mockery. 'Then that's you.' He jabbed at the shepherd, so busy staring vacantly into the sky he'd obviously missed the splash entirely and was quite oblivious of the flock he was supposed to be caring for.

'Hm.' I might have asked for that, but I didn't think I'd been a bad teacher and how could Aled know?

'When I'm set up,' he said, 'you can come and learn you have a country.'

Only then did I understand the contrast he was making between the ploughman's eyes trained to the land and the shepherd's, absently star-gazing.

All I had ever wanted of land was my tiny share of the earth's surface, where I had grown cornflowers because they no longer grew wild. I had never asked for anything so large as a country.

It seemed an age now, since that tiny strip of impoverished soil had gone.

'Cornflowers!' Aled scoffed, tipping his head back against the settle, so that the flaxen hair dropped from around the sallow

128

cheeks. 'Cornflowers to compensate for a country.'

My own hair fell like a grey curtain drawn around my bent head.

He was all the gladness there was left in my life: I could not but be part of the wretchedness of his. As clearly as I saw in him my own roots, he must see in me the withering of his.

No wonder he had so little time for aspiration, when I blocked every outlet of it.

'They compensate even less for loss of health, anyway.'

He sighed deeply, as if sick to death of my endless morbidity, and I felt sick to death of it myself, too. But he said: 'When we're talking I forget how awful these weeks must be for you. But I always think about it afterwards and wonder.'

'Oh Aled, I don't know what these weeks are.' I shifted, restless as his foot stirring again at the unswept ash. 'If things get from bad to worse, I'll look back and think how good they were. And how at peace I was.'

'If you get well, you'll laugh at yourself for feeling so tormented here, and think how depressing we all were.' He tapped the fine white powder, seeming to chide it for not containing what he had sifted through it to find. It flew up around us like a cloud of down from some savaged bird.

'No – d'you know how I'll think of us? As dust. Spinning with the world alright, because we're held in the atmosphere by gravity, but reduced to the smallest particles possible, and released. We would never have met – Ceri and you and me – if we'd still been held by all the normal barriers. So that's how we've bumped into one another – as three specks of dust in a fickle wind that can't diminish us any further.'

All Aled said was: 'I've an idea they might still bury paupers rather than cremate us. Which will put paid to all this senseless hobnobbing.'

'Probably. It's a poor enough sort of immortality to believe in anyway. Poorer than Ceri striking the stars by riding over roof-tops. Or Icarus flying into the sun.'

Aled asked whether I believed in God.

I just said: 'You've got Westminster to blame for what's

129

bugging you,' and left it at that.

We sat for a while watching a lurid green flame caper like some will-o'-the-wisp on a rotten stump.

'Well, eternity's going to be more action-packed than our temporal existence at this rate,' remarked Aled finally, alluding to the wind we could hear getting up outside. Between its spasmodic gusts the trees' soft soughing seemed pained, as though they had no will for the game but yielded indulgently, like ageing adults do with small children who will not give in, but will tug and heave this way and that at them.

But it was cosy in the Hungry Cheese. Ceri's mates were not there – perhaps it was too rough for the bikes, or perhaps they had joined Ceri in the Golden Goose. Most of the men around us were middle-aged – content people, unperturbed by the build-up of the wind: relieved at the break in the weather that seemed imminent, maybe. We all looked well anchored to the place.

'Funny you should say that,' agreed Aled. 'I woke up in the middle of last night wondering whether "The Hungry Cheese" might be a corruption of the French for "the anchor and the chair" – *l'ancre et La chaise*. D'you think it might?'

We asked Thomas, but he didn't know.

'I only manage the fucking place,' he complained.

Then the light went out.

Aled said: 'Must be raining cannon-fodder down the valley,' but he wasn't talking to me: his casual reassurance reached out beyond the feeble fireglow that held the two of us, across the darkness, embracing everyone. 'That cable's got flooded again I bet.'

He was alert to the little flurry of sound from the gloom – his rugged face alive with shadows that played over it like the black patches played over the red, in the picture now invisible on the wall.

The fluster subsided into muttered jokes, but I thought: my God, what's he up to? His hand grasped the back of the settle as he leaned forward, peering, apparently, for some sign of Thomas: then, as if in response to a signal, he got up and crossed beyond the visible.

130

I felt cornered. The Hungry Cheese had never felt such a death-trap – a windowless basement with the only escape-route up two lethal flights of steps – and nothing was easier to engineer than a power-cut. I had an urge to get out while the going was good. But how embarrassing to be caught in flight (or at least, caught gingerly feeling the furniture) – and caught I would surely be, if there was any reason why I should be made to stay. I'd rather not know that, I thought, and the only way of not discovering it, is to sit tight.

He was creeping back: my spine tingled at the outline of him. Conspiratorially he held out to me several sticks of gelignite, laid across his open palm.

I turned the gasp into a cough: candles.

(His hand was indecently big for such a wraith of a man.)

I held them for him to light, but his matchbox contained nothing but the black shreds he had burned through. So we crouched to light them from the embers, nudging the logs with the wicks, like children poking bonfires with sparklers that are slow to catch, on Guy Fawkes' night.

Then we had to melt the bottom ends, to stick them to the saucers he had brought.

And Thomas came eventually with matches.

I took them round the tables, hopelessly awkward at the men's undue thanks, and in a mess with the hot, dripping wax of the cheap things. The oldest man there cupped his hands around the flame as I set it down, careful as a child that knows its own gaucheness, tenderly, as though, deprived of light, he felt the need for warmth. Or as though it was a fragile thing that he had to protect.

And indeed, a draught *was* coming from somewhere – down the steps, I supposed, for it was lifting the coconut matting and setting the candles nearest the door flinching, as if they could hardly bear to look on what they lit up.

As was quite understandable. For everything, and all of us – faces, walls, everything – looked pitted and dented and battered, as though dragged roughly out of some line of fire; as I remembered goods on sale during the war – 'bomb-damaged'. But salvaged.

I watched the red and black shapes on the wall, seeming to wax hot and cold as they expanded and contracted in the uncertainty of the light, and I thought: if they don't come alive for me now, they never will.

'Not long to wait now,' Aled said.

Wait? Wait for what? What was going on? I thought: I knew it, I knew it, but I had no notion what I meant. All that grew clear was my suspicion that Aled had been waiting for this – for the cover of a storm – all the while I had known him. Waiting, day by day, for the weather to break. For the noise, the disruption, the chaos of a storm. To cover what?

He assumed I knew.

'Why don't you take something for it?'

He had caught me rocking to and fro with my jaw cupped in my hands. But he wasn't watching me warily: his eyes, sunk with sleeplessness, were kind.

He must have meant it wasn't long to wait till my operation. Had he meant that?

'Pardon?'

'You were wincing with pain.'

'Everything's wincing – it's the candles.'

'Why don't you?'

'Why don't I what?'

'Take things for it.'

I pointed to the whisky: 'I take that.'

But he hadn't asked it in the way neighbours had asked – implying that if I wouldn't help myself, what could I expect from anyone else? – and I explained that it wasn't that bad, the pain – that it was easier to go along with it than to allow myself to forget it and then plummet into depression each time the drugs began to wear off. I had learnt that having to readjust all the while was harder to bear than the more or less constant, tolerable level of pain I had.

'Yes, perhaps that is easier – going along with things, adapting. . .'

No irony, just sad concession, and a considered pity which didn't seem to irk me any more.

What had happened to all my anger?

I hadn't even got the spark of resistance which had brought me there in the first place, any longer.

'Not long to wait now, anyway.'

'No.' Not long to wait.

An inexorable winding down, before being swallowed into the balm of unconsciousness. The way he said it, he might have been envying me.

Two men got up to go, nodding at Aled. A gust tore down the steps, catching the tray Thomas carried and felling the drinks like skittles. Jumping up to relight a candle for him, I incurred his wrath for grinding broken glass into the mats: then match after match went out in the continuing blast. He commanded and cursed the customers still struggling with the door.

Aled had curled soundlessly as smoke round the screen behind the settle: his calm voice up at the door undercut all Thomas's stridency. '*Nos da,*' the two men called down to us, with the affection of prisoners pausing in their flight to acknowledge the friends left behind to bear the furore of their escape.

You would almost have thought we did expect repercussions. Thomas swept up the glass with delicate restraint, as though its clinking might attract the thunder we could all hear in the distance, and the old man, whose cupped flame had been extinguished despite all his care, moaned in apprehension until Aled swathed the shaking shoulders in his own jacket.

He grasped Aled's hand in the two of his, shaking it up and down with the same troubled need for comfort as I had rocked to and fro.

'If we're ever remembered, it'll probably be for something petty and pointless like that,' was Aled's rueful comment. The sad, grey eyes were touched as the old man's, but I could say nothing. There was nothing of me – not one act, not one thought, petty and pointless or otherwise – that would survive me. I was not even young enough to regret that there wasn't. For there was nothing to be done about it now. Already, behind the flesh of my lips, the bone was eaten away.

Aled's cynicism reasserted itself in an afterthought: 'Of course it's just a symptom of senility, that – disproportionate gratitude. What's the matter?'

I had laughed. 'It's nice you don't think of me as senile anyway.'

For a second he was puzzled; then he saw I was recalling my ingratitude after being rescued from the farmer, and even candle-light couldn't conceal his blush. We were far from being, as yet, atoms in the rain of dust hugging a star.

It was nerve-wracking, waiting down there for the next bout of thunder, beyond the reach of the warning flashes. And it was only when we heard the chimney spitting into the fire that we knew the rain had started.

But what everyone took to be hailstones, Aled and I could see was mortar crumbling from inside the chimney and washed down onto the logs. Thomas noticed it too, and at each flush of it he would turn quickly as if to startle and arrest it (much as though he was playing 'wolf' in a children's game).

It ended in a deluge that put the fire out. We all glanced to where the chimney-breast joined the ceiling, as if expecting a hole to suddenly gape. No-one made any move to relight the fire. The pyramid of mortar globules in the hearth smoked a little, wistfully, then resigned themselves to doing without bricks.

Over the wind, I heard tearing – a gradual, personal, isolating roar that filled my head. The tearing of the tumour again as my tooth was pulled. Pain shot across my mouth, and it filled with fluid.

Then, crashing. In the real world. The crashing of sea around the Hungry Cheese, with the dyke-gates burst open and the keeper drunk.

In slow motion, the beer-barrel table toppling, and Aled rising. The ceiling, the ceiling: but Aled and Thomas stared unheeding at the steps. A slow, heavy sighing as the crashing died.

I swallowed, but it was only saliva.

Thomas and Aled exchanged curt words and fled up the steps, Aled calling: 'Tree's down' sharply to us.

The candle had slid off our barrel and ignited the mat: flames spurted in a little circle, through which the liquid wax oozed. I stamped at them, only then noticing the faster spread of the smouldering beyond them – smouldering that scurried like chicks among the undergrowth while the parent birds flapped and danced and distracted the intruder's attention.

Tree? Of course – that huge old oak across the road, whose shadow I had seen a hundred times reach out vainly, hungrily, to the steps of the pub.

'Has it jammed the door?' I asked quickly as Aled reappeared for an instant.

'It's burst it open.' He paused, thrown off his stride by my lack of common sense. Then he surveyed the others, assessing them, and they looked to him, but half warily, for he was only human, and although he would not desert them, there was no knowing what he would have them do.

I hadn't noticed it get so cold.

'Can't we get out that way?' There was a door behind the bar, I remembered now.

'You want to spend the rest of your life in the bogs?' Aled was getting equal to my idiocy.

I had always thought it was a way through into the hotel.

Thomas must spend a phenomenal amount of time in the toilet.

Aled said: 'I'll get out and ring the fire-brigade.' Thomas demurred. I thought: typical – you get a hotel caked up to the hilt with fire-precautions and its pub has one entrance: no wonder Thomas doesn't want the fire-brigade. It suddenly struck me that the dance-hall had only one entrance, too, even if it was from the fire-escape. What a place! But Aled was off.

I charged up the steps after him, curious merely. The door was askew, wrenched off its top hinge, and a mass of foliage and branches protruded like some rampant tropical jungle crushing the traces of our ruined civilisation; imprisoning us in them.

'How will you ever get through that?'

He writhed into it like a snake, and slowly the vegetation stopped heaving and settled, and it was as if the last ripples had dispersed from where Aled had drowned.

At least we could now see when lightning struck.

Thomas, rising to the occasion at last, was distributing free drink. But there was no sign of any more candles, to replace the ones getting dangerously low.

The jungle jostled – but it wasn't a man in uniform. It was Aled, emerging like some parody of Tarzan, armed with a torch and a hatchet. *'Dyw'r ffôn ddim yn gweithio.'*

I held the torch while he hacked, alternately standing at the door raining blind blows at the branches, and climbing up where he could see and reach but had no freedom to manoeuvre. Disgruntled with both methods, he was changing from one to the other with increasing impatience when the old man still draped in his jacket came urgently up to us. Seeing he stood little chance of getting Aled's attention, he told me in English that we should climb out the chimney. Thomas, bringing up whiskies behind him, managed to deflect him to the chimney by pretending to take him seriously.

Aled stopped to watch, critically, as they staggered together down the steps. I wondered what he thought of the free flow of drink, in view of the imminent ascent through the wrecked head of a sideways oak.

'At least there's only six of us,' I said, forgetting Thomas, and not counting Aled.

Aled looked at the ugly truncated limb beside him with misgivings – as though it would stake us all.

He said something I could not catch for the wind in the leaves, but he didn't repeat it – he just leant down to touch the torch, to remind me to train it to where he worked. The hatchet seemed hopelessly blunt.

I found I could help by holding back the branches as he hacked – opening the wounds as he made them.

He stopped to decide whether we should climb up into the tree or stick to our footing on the steps and wriggle through.

The steps were knee-deep in smashed debris.

I indicated 'up' with the torch and he nodded, the sweat shining on his face. He pointed to his jaw, questioningly.

I remembered I had told him that cold aggravated the pain.

I wrinkled my face in unconcern and grinned encouragement at the grotesque amputations around him.

He was, actually, making a right hash of the job.

136

I touched the tip of the axe and rolled my eyes: he blew his cheeks out and shook his head in weariness, and hacked on.

The closer he came to securing a way out, the more he was letting the weather in.

I thought: when this torch gets soaked it will go out.

Aled was so wet he seemed to bleed quite profusely from the scratches he was given by the resilient twigs he kept twisting irritably out of his way.

There was what sounded like a landslide behind us.

'Chimney?' mouthed Aled, but neither of us went to look.

He must have thought that if he were much longer everyone would need rescuing from the top of the roof instead of the basement, for he went at the oak with such unexpected vehemence that I lost control momentarily over the illuminations.

Thomas came to see how we were getting on: I saw Aled notice it was he who was wearing his jacket now.

'What are they playing at down there? Charades?'

In my opinion, he ought to have been thankful the thing was not compounded with soot.

When I went down to tell them to come up, I found the room coated in a thick layer of plaster-dust, intricately patterned with footprints and fingerprints.

We were leaving a place that looked as though it had been stampeded.

But they were orderly enough. Aled had climbed into the tree and stationed himself at the point we were to climb to and then traverse from. Tentatively, he beckoned to me.

But I pointed to the torch.

They sent up the old man who had had designs on the chimney, first, which might have been a mistake. He had no sooner been given a leg-up than he struck out along an impossible deviation.

I made it quite plain that I would shine the torch nowhere except along the planned route.

But it was Aled who, by dint of deliberate non-comprehension, lured him to a spot where he could lift him like a child by the armpits and thrust him out into the world.

The second nearly injured himself by letting go in a flash of lightning.

137

Three, four, easy.

Then the most jovial, earnest as he was clumsy, struggling too hard, too heavy to help. He stopped, shaking with fear, to show us oak-apples. When he froze, Aled gave him precise directions. 'Right foot four inches higher. That's only two. Yes, that's it.'

Then Thomas.

I tried to usher him past. 'Oh, get on up woman,' he pleaded with the profound exasperation of someone who has been restraining himself from time immemorial.

'Then hold this and shine it properly.' I was forgetting I was in a skirt.

Thomas was mercilessly obedient.

'Bloody shoes,' I gasped as Aled grabbed, to break my fall. He said nothing: there was nothing in his face: he did not look at me.

Thomas was not long after me.

The moment I saw his head rise from the foliage, it struck me we could be out in the storm for the rest of the night. 'Have you got the key to the revolving doors?' I shouted urgently.'

'Jesus. Woman,' he said. Really swearing at me. For no reason at all.

I gave up, it being apparent there was no way he was going back down for any key.

I took the torch from him to light the way for Aled, but time and again he had jumped lithely out of its beam before I could anticipate him. Whenever they caught up with him, though, the weak rays picked out the yellowish tinge to him, to his head, to his hands; and the yellowish hue, even, of his long-bleached denims, looking as though their thousand washings had been in the muddy pools of the lane, where the young farm children came to stand in wellies, hand in hand, splashing on the edge, quite unperturbed that there was nothing in the world to do.

138

CHAPTER TEN

It was impossible to catch up on sleep the next morning. An uproar of yelling men and blaring cars had been going on for hours when I gave up trying and looked at my watch, and it had only just turned half-past eight then. Thomas, impassively serving breakfast as though nothing was going on outside (never mind all the high jinks during the night) answered my questions in mono-syllables just adequate enough to relay an eight o'clock news item about all roads into the town being impassable, due to flooding and fallen trees.

I reflected, with gloomy irritation, that the motorists must have been striving to get to work with as little success as I had been striving to get to sleep, and that had I hung on a bit, they would have given up and gone home, and there might have been peace.

But motorists, it emerged, were tenacious. When I went down the lane to inspect the damage, it was still on the increase, with drivers refusing to abandon either their plans or their cars at the toppled oak. Distraught men in Council pink were clambering through the tree, remonstrating with the jammed traffic and lopping branches with a circular saw that was now drowning most of the human fracas and internal combustion straining.

Already some of the more massive limbs had been sliced off, and their yellow stumps stared blindly at the dull sky, above the soft mole-hills of their sawdust whirling into the air, light as bone-ash, and depositing a fine film across the windscreens of the intrepid motorists. These were swerving, one after the other, mounting the lesser branches with such force that they twisted as if in agony, scraping the roofs and windows with frantic claws: but the only break in the line was as some driver revved and bounced back and had to rev again.

One vehicle wrenched the flex of the saw, and the shocking-

139

pink men converged on it like ants upon a snout that is probing too far. The saw, I noticed then, was working from an electric point inside the main door of the old farmhouse, which I had always thought defunct. It stood torn ajar like some broken taboo, and into it the live flex snaked.

At the heart of all the commotion lay the tree, like the corpse of some stranded mammoth, being mutilated and hauled apart and dumped half upon the hedge. Only the obdurately clinging ivy looked alive, for under such onslaught the leaves had been prematurely shed and the stark twigs stuck out piercingly as hands lifted from acid baths.

The road was carpeted with the half-turned foliage; it was tending to obscure hazards like discarded tools and severed limbs.

Later in the morning they rigged up traffic-lights there.

At lunch-time I went back again: the workmen had knocked off and I was struck by how neat and clean and smooth all their official excisions were, compared with Aled's rough midnight hacking around the doorway of the Hungry Cheese.

There was no way it would open for lunch.

I walked down the road for a while, but it was cold and my jaw ached, and though the wind had dropped it hadn't died. It plucked at me as it plucked at the half-stripped hedgerows and at the trees, standing everywhere in attitudes of shock at their own nakedness.

The night had brought winter with a vengeance.

By evening, the entrance to the Hungry Cheese was clear and I helped Thomas clean up there, and when Aled did not appear I began to wonder if the caravans at the Abbey had been reduced to matchwood.

The next day I thought I would go and find out, and I got almost as far as the riverbank. But then I was faced with a stretch of swamp and I turned back. If there was anything I could do, he knew where to find me.

Obviously there was nothing I could do. He couldn't have missed me, for I was in the Hungry Cheese from opening time to closing time. The red and black shapes still on the wall multiplied without restraint. I got rather drunk there.

When I heard the bang in the night I couldn't wake up. And I assumed the roaring and the bright flickering light were in my head. Some time must have passed before I was standing at the window watching a fire burning through a hole in the farmhouse roof.

There was something about it that was not convincing.

The flames were flapping rather absurdly, as if they had been superimposed on a film set. Red flames, quite thin, even transparent. Two-dimensional. But also, too extravagant; too hysterical; too like Hollywood.

And the chimney was moving.

Hangover, I thought, or maybe the shimmerings of hot air. But then it creased up, like a face about to burst into tears. And then it fell, coiling neatly, in slow motion, crumbling like cake into the hole – into the wild, rip-roaring furnace. Never, surely, a real chimney.

I closed my eyes for the pain in my head; and when I opened them people had been sketched in. Two animated paper cut-outs below the flames, on the top-floor fire-escape; running in opposite directions; running together again as though on elastic. I felt inclined to laugh.

But one of them was leaning over the rail as if he was vomiting. 'No, no,' I shouted, flinging open the window, but I was calling to figures on celluloid. There was nothing for it but to watch him jump.

Then the fire-alarm went. Splitting my head. On and on; tearing round and round the yard like some trapped madman.

An official fire. Certified.

I remember stubbing my big toe hard on the bed: I remember a sudden wave of heat: I remember the jumble of yesterday's clothes on the wicker chair: I remember the pounding of feet tearing past down the corridor.

'Wait, wait.'

But nobody waited, and nobody came back.

My petticoat slithered from the chair, so I left it; and when my right foot got strangled in the left leg of my tights, I didn't bother with them any more, either.

It got suddenly brighter and I looked up. The flames had turned

141

yellow. They were full-bodied and earnest and angry now.

The fire-escape was bare.

Bra not fastening: was it quicker to struggle with it as it was, or to take it off and start again, right side out?

'Excuse us – sorry, sorry.'

Two boys, starkers, coming in the window. Shouting. Wanting something.

'Sorry, but there's. . .'

'What?'

'Sorry – there's. . .'

'What?'

'Fire.'

'Yes.'

'Sorry – we got caught. Can we. . .?'

'Yes, yes.' I waved impatiently at the door. They were losing all the time they would save by the short-cut.

'Thanks.' He tugged at my bedspread.

'What?'

'Borrow – sorry – thanks.' Shoulder-blades to make you wince.

'Oh yes of course – sorry.'

'Sorry. Thanks.'

The one behind grabbed the top blanket.

'Thanks. OK? Sorry.' He had shoes on, that one, shoes out of all proportion to the scrawny little ankles.

They seemed nervous, suspicious of what I was clutching so determinedly behind my back. I could have wished it was something more than two unattached bits of elastic.

Decently swaddled, the boys tottered back onto the fire-escape like geisha-girls.

One minced back.

'You'd better come too.'

'Yes, yes, alright, I'm coming – you get on.'

But they came rushing back in as I chased after them, and we collided.

'God!'

'Sorry – there's. . .'

'What?'

142

'Sorry. Burning stuff falling everywhere.'

'Oh – can't you. . .?

'No. Sorry. Can we. . .?

'What?'

'This way. . .?' They were sneaking towards the door.

'That's what I thought you wanted in the first place.'

'Oh. Sorry.'

'Well, just make your minds up,' I bawled.

Outside, windows were popping, like cooking eyeballs.

The smoke in the corridor surprised me.

A soft grey wall of it at the corner, with trails of it floating towards us like ringlets loosened from their bandaging. As we hovered, coughing came from behind it, like the coughing of sheep through a mist, luring us there somehow.

Thinking of mist, I was unprepared for the shock of not being able to breathe.

I wondered, in panic, whether Aled would hear screaming above the wail of the siren.

After that it was impossible to scream for the urgency of hacking and retching. Whenever I paused to suck in smoke, I heard the awful noise of the others' choking.

I knew from the buffetting on either side, that all three of us were on our knees.

It got so that it was hard not to be sick.

Whizzing glass and plummetting fire-brands seemed a small price to pay for air.

I made a dash for it and the smoke seemed to thin and we hurtled through a door onto the fire-escape, gulping at the fresh air as though it were water and we dying of thirst. Even so, we still couldn't stop coughing.

My throat was so painful every cough was agony.

We were flat-out, too flat-out to react to the shower of sparks that landed on us.

Lying on the platform, I could hear tiles detonating in the yard below.

The two boys were propped up against the wall, drooping under my bedclothes like things draped for spring-cleaning.

I all but divested one, pushing him ahead of me along the balcony; the other clung to me from behind and we proceeded to the spiralling steps in the shaky manner of a trio flung off the end in a rather too hectic session of the rumba.

On the way past my room, I nipped in for a towel, having developed some peculiar yen for one since I had last set foot there.

Fortunately, the youngsters showed no sign of realising I hadn't got them very far. The less inert was preoccupied with the bedspread, none the more glamorous for having slipped from his bony shoulders. Instead of hitching the thing up, he kept pulling it more tightly around him, increasing its tendency to trip him up.

I saw for the first time that his hair was burnt, charred, and the back of his neck an angry red, with blisters coming.

I had assumed they were nude because they had dashed, in the thoughtless manner of youth, straight from bed. But now I wondered.

And I marvelled they could look so much skinnier than they had ever looked in the Hungry Cheese, despite always wearing skin-tight clothes there. It must have been the studding that had given the illusion of muscle.

The one in the lead was so white and corpse-like it was strange to see his bare feet bleed as we fled across the glass in the yard, bombarded by meteors from the blazing sky.

But when I glanced back, from under the archway into the lane, it was all like some circus act. The flames, far more widespread now, were licking at the stars like a pride of lions leaping at some prey safely out of reach.

So many people were running up and down the lane that I hesitated about which way to turn. Then I was caught up in the crush, and it wasn't until I was swept out into the back road that I realised I had lost the lads.

They must have run the other way, away from the fuss.

The road was teeming.

It was as if bees had been smoked out of the honeycomb. There was a frantic swarming around the flashing lights of police cars, around the fire-engine.

I tried to get across the road, to join a group I could see waiting

144

in the roadside, standing quietly, with the regulation hotel towels slung around their necks or over their half-clothed shoulders or arms, or trailing listlessly from their hands.

I made my own towel obvious as I came up to them, as though it were the sign by which I expected to be recognised, and accepted.

Whoever would have guessed there were so many of us to be flushed out from the cracks and pores of that hollow old building?

The few remains of the oak that had still not been carted away lay beside us like the indigestible parts of some devoured creature.

Standing at my side was a bulky man, more clad than most, patiently, passively watching the flames spreading to the modern wing.

'That must have been some really freak lightning.' I betrayed the anxious enthusiasm of a child that needed reassuring.

The massive head inclined with slow contempt to his elbow. 'Lightning be damned,' he drawled viciously.

A second fire-engine arrived.

And another police car.

As they drew up they switched off their sirens, and then we could hear again, from inside the hotel, the fire-alarm, eerie as some feeble cry for help from a trapped victim we had abandoned there.

It was the kind of noise that could almost have been imaginary.

A fireman, exposed on a small platform, had been swung aloft on a crane to the level of the flames.

Not far from us two others clutched at a nozzle, struggling to train the jet onto the blaze. But forceful as it was at the roadside, it seemed to disperse and virtually evaporate before reaching the roof.

Then Thomas was there, ushering us further down the road like some mother hen. The man at my side tried to start an argument, but Thomas was soothing, patting backs, and resting his hands on the shoulders of women. He was presented with a towel or two, and somehow he ended up coming round collecting the lot. It was like some Tibetan ceremony. 'Are you alright?' he asked when he caught sight of me, bending anxiously to single me out, as though, for a second, I was the only person in the world that mattered.

145

My bare feet were sticking, very uncomfortably, to the insides of my shoes.

The jet from the top of the crane attacked the flames strongly and directly and altogether more hopefully.

Remembering what Aled called the attics, I thought: well, they're 'glory holes' alright now.

I supposed he would see the fire from the caravans.

The flames were less high, but they were glowing behind new windows on the second floor.

The police had managed to establish a kind of front line of onlookers.

Ceri!

I was shouted at from several directions for treading on a hose: it made me dither and I trod on it again: a fireman strode forward and roughly wheeled me about, but I dodged under his arm and across the road.

'Ceri, Ceri, you're OK?' What was more, he was fully dressed.

Why on earth I should feel overcome I had no idea, unless I'd been imagining the conflagration as the climax of his legendary ride across the rooftops.

But he was overcome too: didn't seem to mind my hand on his arm: grasped it, shook hands with me impetuously. Nothing for it in the end but to revert to inadequate, traditional gestures.

'I thought you. . . I thought. . . I wasn't sure. I'm glad you're alright.'

'And I'm glad of your hair, Ceri – I wouldn't have found you.'

But he was trying to say something else. 'Were you. . .? You weren't. . .? In there. . .?' He was getting nervy, his glance flitting away, and a dismay of embarrassment taking over.

'I got out alright,' I reassured him calmly, thinking: the poor boy will no doubt have to go through all this embarrassment again with his mother.

But it wasn't embarrassment. It was blankness. His face had gone like the faces of the two naked lads I had lost. Blank and a little scared: like children who cannot comprehend why they have been punished so hard.

I thought: what the hell am I going to say to Thomas about

146

where my bedclothes have gone?

Suddenly, silence.

The stopping of the hotel's fire-alarm was as chilling as the switching-off of a life-support machine.

But Thomas was hearty. He came bustling over, his arms outstretched to embrace us, to embrace the world. It was arranged we should all go to a school for the night: mattresses were being organised, so was breakfast: mini-buses would take us there. How could I ever have thought him a pathetic coward, when he was like this, and his hotel burning to the ground behind him?

It did not burn to the ground: in fact there turned out to be relatively little damage other than to the top floor and attics of the old wing. When I went back to my room it was as I had left it, except that everything was covered with grime, and the texture of the curtains had changed, as though the plastic had softened and then hardened again, more brittle than before.

Aled, alone, was dead.

We were let back in, but only to collect our things. I worked methodically round the room, picking up as though they were articles from another planet, my clothes, my shoes, my washing things, smearing the greasy film that coated them all.

The bomb he had been making had blown up on him.

We had watched the toy-like fireman in the sky being lowered into the gaping hole; watched him disappear with the pang of watching a coffin sink into the flames.

And we had watched him reappear, a figure on a clockface when the hour is struck, making, mechanically, with his two gloved hands, the wide, flat gesture, 'no'.

I'd overheard a policeman's satisfied comment: 'The bomber's got his come-uppance then,' and I'd guessed.

It explained Ceri's relief at seeing me.

Or did it?

I still didn't know whether he was affected because he thought I'd been blown up with Aled, or because, seeing me, he thought Aled would be alive too.

I was only beginning to unravel the ironies of what had happened.

Like the irony of my suspiciousness. It might have led me to think something was going on, but it had also led me to suppose 'fertilizer' must be the code-name for something horrendous, instead of straight-forward fertilizer, out of which bombs could be made.

And the irony that it had not been Aled or Ceri who had first aroused my suspicions, but Thomas. It had been his lying and false implying, and the impression he gave of concealing a secret part of his life deliberately badly because he despised it.

What would he say to everyone now?

He would tell them, I supposed, the bare bones of what had happened to his hotel, quashing all their sympathetic horror and indignation by a gruff dismissiveness.

Quashing too, perhaps, under the same dismissiveness, other sympathies of his own that it was not quite the done thing to feel.

I locked my suitcase and I carried it downstairs. I handed the key of my room over to Thomas and I stood by, awkwardly and guiltily, while he meticulously counted out the deposit to return to me.

He said nothing, nor did he look at me.

But I happened to catch his eyes as I was spinning towards him on the second circuit that his revolving doors always seemed to require of me, and the disgust with which he was watching my desertion gave his face some fleeting semblance of dignity.

I wondered if he would go to prison.

I half tumbled onto the dazzlingly bright pavement, much as Alice must have emerged from behind the looking glass.

When you have been waiting, nowhere in particular, for five weeks and five days, it only takes a bus-ride to make your pulse race.

And all that time of preparation is nothing, is wasted, as you hurtle down the motorway, excitedly urging the coach to go faster, faster, to obliterate all the people in rooms in houses in terraces on outskirts, and let you succumb to the pure thrill of speed.

But we didn't drive fast enough for that oblivion, and I was left clutching at the night's life beyond the flyovers; the rows of streetlights throbbing like arteries, curving, crossing, threading and joining more and more intricately as we approached the fearful heart of the city. All of it, civilised life, working in harmony: a miracle of organisation, like a human body: how on earth was it all organised? And how was I here, being sucked into the organisation, sucked into the streams of people that would be rushing up and down the platforms, the lifts, the corridors, the wards, the operating theatre? Surely it was stronger than me, all this miracle of organisation absorbing me – far, far stronger! And infinitely stronger, surely, than one insignificant tumour scraping away at one tiny corner of me! Just as it had been infinitely stronger than what had gnawed at Aled.

And yet how frail it all was, too. How did they last, those tiny orange bulbs strung like necklaces around the throat of the city? How could they last? Horribly, horribly exposed tubes of frail glass, buffetted by all the weathers that the heavens could send. Hopelessly vulnerable, pin-pricking for a second the eternal darkness of space.

They were reflected everywhere, those tiresome lights: there they lay in the wet road: there they were daubing the shining bodies of the columns of traffic zooming, crawling, interlacing around us: and there they were in the sky we looked out at, multiplied into constellation upon constellation of shooting stars. There was no getting away from them.

To them, I belonged; only to them. They were what it was to be human, and they were all that being human was, and to them, I prayed to cling. Not for any future, for there is none, but simply for all of this, dear God, oh let me be alright, let me be alright, let me be alright.

It is a base instinct, the will to survive.